CONN

JANE FRASER lives, works and writes fiction in a house facing the sea in the Gower peninsula, south Wales. In 2017 she was a finalist for the Manchester Fiction Prize and in 2018 was a prize-winner for the Fish Memoir Prize and selected as a Hay Festival Writer at Work. In 2022, she was commissioned by BBC Radio 4 for the first time to write a short story which was broadcast as part of its *Short Works* series. In 2022, she was also awarded The Paul Torday Memorial Prize for her debut novel, *Advent*. She has a PhD in Creative Writing from Swansea University, is wife to Philip and co-director of NB:Design, a business they share, and importantly, grandmother to Megan, Florence and Alice.

JANE FRASER

CONNECTIVE TISSUE

SALT
MODERN
STORIES

SALT

CROMER

PUBLISHED BY SALT PUBLISHING 2022

2 4 6 8 10 9 7 5 3 1

First published in Great Britain in 2022 by
Salt Publishing Ltd
12 Norwich Road, Cromer, Norfolk NR27 0AX United Kingdom

www.saltpublishing.com

Salt Publishing Limited Reg. No. 5293401

A CIP catalogue record for this book is available from the British Library

ISBN 978 1 78463 252 6 (Paperback edition)
ISBN 978 1 78463 253 3 (Electronic edition)

Typeset in Granjon by Salt Publishing

Printed and bound in Great Britain by Clays Ltd, St Ives plc

*To my husband, Philip, for his constant support
and honest criticism of my work.*

Contents

CONNECTIVE TISSUE

The Sausage Maker's Daughter

M Y BED VIBRATES with the force of the chopping down below. An alarm call of sorts. Six o'clock on the dot, six days a week and Dad's already marking time with monotonous thuds, his maple block bowing in the middle with the weight of the years. There's comfort in the rhythm, and the smell of sweet meat that pervades this house above the shop.

As usual there's no stirring from Mum in the bedroom at the front. Dad tells me she likes to have a little lie in of a morning, that she hasn't had it easy what with one thing and the other. So at eight o'clock Dad leaves his chopping for just long enough to bring us both a cup of tea so that we can come-to nicely. He takes Mum a Marie biscuit to settle her stomach. He asks if I'd like a slice of toast when I come down, but I'd better not be too long as he has to open up at nine. It's Saturday. *They'll be queuing outside the door*, he laughs, *shopping bags at the ready*. He tells me Mum's having one of her days so she's going to have a bit of a rest, stay put. I tell him I'll give him a hand in the shop. At sixteen what else might I be doing?

Dad sets me a place at the red Formica table with the drop leaves in the back kitchen. I sit on the old settle but he stands with his back to the Rayburn, as if he's trying to absorb enough warmth into his body to keep him going. His hands are always so cold, fridge-cold, tinged blue at the nails, cut short and scrubbed clean. I have the urge to cry as I look at him in his freshly starched white coat, his blue and white striped apron on top, ties crossed at the back, wrapped around him twice, and double-knotted at the front.

"Why's she not getting up again, then?" I ask.

"Leave it now," he says, "no point in getting all worked up about things."

Don't go upsetting your mother is the mantra we live by in this strange house where Mum is the semi-present butcher's wife, who spends half her life tucked up in flannelette sheets, curtains drawn tight against the rows of identical grey, terraced houses.

I clear the dishes for Dad and then walk along the long, dark passage towards the shop. The frosted glass door that separates it from the house is three-quarters open. It's kept ajar by a large, iron meat-hook that hangs from the stainless steel bar suspended from the ceiling. Dad likes to keep the door open so that he can keep an eye on things, listen out for any movement if, and when, it comes.

Once inside, I greet the carcasses he's had delivered from the local slaughter house. There's a side of beef, the lights, hearts and kidneys of the scarf attached; a pig, snout down, front trotters crossed, remains of bristles and hair that have escaped the scald and the shave visible; and two skinned lambs.

I glance at the round walnut clock above the door: one minute to.

"Better let them in before they break the door down," he says.

I unbolt the shop door, top and bottom, pull up the white blind. There's no one waiting on the other side, just the empty pavement and the rain nailing down. I reverse the sign from *closed*, written in black by Dad's magic marker, to *open*, written in red.

Armed with an empty liver tin, I climb up onto the white marble slab inside the shop front and unhook the sheets of greaseproof paper that hang from a brass bar running the full length of this window to the world. I place the hooks carefully into the tin. *One hook, two sheets,* says Dad. *Overlap them. Don't waste.* I smooth each of the ten sheets into a pile and put them in the back room ready to be used again at closing time whatever time that might be, when Dad says: *That's it. Don't think there'll be anyone else now.*

"Shall I do a bit of a display?" I ask.

"You can try," he says. "Stuff's in the cold room."

I turn the handle to raise the iron bar and heave open the dense door of the walk-in fridge. The automatic light comes on inside. Even though I should be used to it by now, I'm afraid the door will slam behind me, the light will go out, sealing me in the chilled darkness. Recently the fear is more intense.

I leave the heavy stuff for Dad, but as for the stainless steel trays with the beef pieces all cut up into evenly sized cubes, the loin chops and the minced beef, I can carry those.

What would I do without you? Dad says every day. *Especially the way things are.* I trundle the trays back and fore to the shop window, position them in the hope that they'll catch the customer's eye. The passing trade.

When I've done that I ferry what Dad calls the *extras* so they're in full view of the street: homemade faggots, pressed tongue, brawn, the roast pork that he's wrapped in foil and lovingly tended in the Rayburn, crisped the crackling in the top oven to finish off.

He tells me not to forget the burgers. He's invested in a little manual press lately, circles of greaseproof paper to separate the finely ground beef – *no muck in these like the bloody new-fangled supermarkets are selling. Tesco won't last,* he goes on. *You mark my words.*

In the back room of the shop, he works late into the evenings, pressing out the burgers in defence of his corner shop, a lonely one-man assembly line. As he keeps telling me, it's all he's ever known. And when he's done with that, he stuffs raw sausage meat and a little rusk into the barrel of a red iron sausage-making machine and gently eases the emerging pink meat out of the metal tube like toothpaste into the white-lace intestines of lambs. Try as I might, I can't loop the sausages like Dad. *It's easy,* he says, *just press and twist.* But it isn't easy. Any of it.

I finish off my window display with a length of Raymond Williams' famed homemade sausages, draped from a hook. In between the sparkle and shine of the steel trays, I place imitation orange-red tomatoes and lime-green plastic lettuce leaves. But I doubt if this will change things.

Behind the counter, facing the wall, we stand at our blocks. He has the large one for chopping, dissecting, slicing

– the intricate work, and I have an offspring version for the small stuff that's not too dangerous: liver and the like which I can slice and weigh on the Avery scales. When I've done that I wrap in greaseproof paper and then enclose in a single sheet of yesterday's newspapers which I've cut along the folds with one of Dad's knives. They dazzle against the shiny, white surface of the tiles of the wall behind the block, left to right in ascending order of blade-size: six inchers, seven inchers, ten and twelve inchers, straight blades, curved blades, scimitars, skinners, boners and breakers. He likes to keep things in order, everything in its place, where it should be, where it's always been.

I watch him as he peels back the fat with a knife to expose the aged flesh of beef beneath. He throws the trimmings into a large meat tray on the floor, ready to boil and make dripping once it's full again. The rusty smell doesn't bother us at all, though it's not to everyone's taste the way it's always in the air. Gets under the skin, Mum says. Can never wash the grease completely out of Dad's apron however hard she tries.

He works with concentration, pride even, etched into his face which is looking a lot older than his forty-two years. He deals with the sinew and the tendons, gets rid of the guts and the offal. Then he breaks down the beast into its named and manageable parts just like the jigsaw diagram of the cow in the alcove: topside, silverside, hind quarter and forequarter. He moves around the dead animal like the Master Butcher he is. He has a certificate to prove it hanging on the wall and a sign in an old-fashioned font, full of loops and swirls, above the shop front outside, for all the world to see: Raymond Williams Purveyor of Fine Meats.

"Did you ever want to do anything else apart from being a butcher?" I ask.

"Never had the chance," he says, "had to come out of school at fourteen to help with the business after the war."

"And what if the war hadn't happened? What if David hadn't been killed?"

"Surgeon, I think. Passed the 11+, you know. Not much difference really between a surgeon and a butcher."

"Only the money," I say.

"Yes. Only the money," he says. "Things might have been different then."

He slices up the sirloins and puts them in an orderly row in the tray in the window, stabbing one of the thick steaks with a price sign that says 7s/6d per pound.

"What's really wrong with her, Dad?" I ask.

"Up and down a bit, that's all. What with the business being slow. She's not one for change, your mother. Likes the *idea* of being in business. All she's ever known, see," he says.

"Can't go on like this, Dad," I say.

"No choice. Pity she hadn't married that bloody dentist," he says. "Called it off because he was always telling her what to do. Doesn't like being told, your mother."

We stop talking as we hear the creak of the stair treads. We turn from the blocks as Mum wafts into the shop. She's dressed up to the nines in her pale-blue two-piece and matching court shoes and bag, her dark hair coiffed, and made-up and ready for the off. I smell her distinctive Yardley perfume as she click-clacks past the counter. It smells out of place among the sweet stench of dead meat.

"Up and about, then?" Dad says, smiling. "Feeling a bit better?"

"Mmm . . . thought I'd go into town for a couple of hours, have a little look around the shops," she says.

"Go you, love. Give yourself a bit of a fillip," says Dad. "Get yourself something nice."

I give her one of my looks; but she doesn't respond.

She totters around to our side of the counter and offers us each, in turn, her cheek to kiss before opening the till. In goes her gloved hand, deep into the back of the drawer, reaching for the car-keys and a couple of fivers.

It's here in the compartments at the back, beyond the notes and the coins, that Dad keeps his precious things safe: the last letter from his brother before he was shot down, my first milk tooth, a curl from my hair, and a black and white picture of his wedding. In the frozen image, their skin is unlined, their lips upturned.

"See you later," she says.

After she's gone we stand together behind the counter; waiting mostly. From time to time I glance at the clock, wondering when Dad will decide to shut up shop so I can hook the sheets of greaseproof paper back up and block the world out for the weekend. He keeps smiling at me and saying: *Well, you can't call it busy, but it's steady. Give it just a little while longer.*

Stragglers from the grey, rain-drenched neighbourhood come in dribs and drabs, wanting little except a handful of mince, a half a pound of sausages, a packet of dripping, the odd burger. Some want nothing more than a bag of bones for the dog, a scrag end, the left-overs.

Blackberries

I USED TO believe that sometimes things could be too perfect, that when life was going well, perhaps too well, it just couldn't last. It was just a fear, I suppose – though I did once hear a tale of a teenage boy called Evans who apparently had it all: good looks, athleticism, charm – you know the type. Anyway, he fell out of a tree performing some prank, days before his sixteenth birthday and that was the end of Evans. Though this story was told to me decades ago, it somehow stayed with me, springing up on me every now and then, usually when I was perhaps a little too smug about life, as though to hold me in check and give me a little warning.

I was oiling the five-bar farm-gate in my garden with *Ronseal* Teak Oil when these thoughts last came back to me. Perhaps they drifted in on the summer breeze that hot August afternoon. It was an unusual breeze come to think of it, easterly, off the land, dry and pollen-laden – so different from the damp, salt-laden south-westerlies that usually buffeted these parts. I remember the breeze caressing my uncovered shoulders, noticing the fine hairs, bleached blond by the sun, stand up on my bare, outstretched arms which, I recall thinking, were almost the same colour as the gate I was brushing; a rich teak. I remember feeling vital. Yes, that's the word. My new husband had told me I was blooming. I remember taking a few minutes to acknowledge how happy I was and to be grateful for it. My life had recently started over again and I was hungry for everything. For relishing my work and piano playing and gardening and growing organic vegetables and learning Welsh and running miles each day along the beach. I was blessed.

And this feeling I breathed in along with the vapour of the teak oil, the turps in the pot on the grass, the coconut oil I'd rubbed into my skin and the honeysuckle that had started to creep through the hedges in the lane outside. Along with the honeysuckle crept simple tales and folk-lore. You couldn't seem to escape these in the country; *don't cast a clout 'til may is out*; *red sky at morning, shepherd's warning*, and the one about blackberries which I couldn't exactly recall but which my mother had told me, in a chilling voice, when I was a child, something about never daring to touch those that hung on the hedges after Calan Gaeaf for fear they'd be touched by the Devil's spit. I particularly remember then how I was drawn to those blackberries, the white flowers still clinging to the firm, green fruit of the unripened flesh at their centre and anticipating how ripe and juicy they'd be by autumn when they'd be mine for the taking. And that's when Evans came back to me.

The off-shore breezes continued all week and every day the temperature rose. It was said to be one of the hottest summers on record. It didn't seem possible it could get any hotter. But it did. Strange though, as it *sounded* like winter, especially in the early mornings and towards dusk when the wind got up and moaned eerily. It felt foreign, sultry, almost unreal. And I loved it; the strangeness of it. Loved the way the trees spoke in a different way, whispering almost. Loved the way the sea sounded nearer than normal, echoing through the stillness. Loved the shafts of sunlight burrowing into my skin and bones. I knew it wouldn't last and I wanted my fill of it, and would lie stretched out in the full glare of the afternoon sun on the hot slabs of the patio, a cat, almost purring with ecstasy in a state of semi-consciousness, letting my imagination drift. And there I'd lie languid, until I was sapped and wilting like the summer blooms, in the parched flowers beds, their heads drooping, desperate for a shower of rain to breathe life into them once more.

By the weekend, I sensed a change; by late afternoon on the Saturday, the stillness was oppressive, ominously calm. The humidity was achingly heavy, the kind of heaviness that made your ankles swell and your limbs drag. The landscape took on a strange hue. I remember thinking how air and earth had become one; even the slate chippings surrounding the lavender bushes seemed to be absorbed into each other and the air which took on a mantle of deep plum, as if it itself had substance and texture. The atmosphere was clouded with irritating bugs; thunder bugs. I could smell the ozone: we were due a storm to clear the air.

It was as dusk descended and the heavens turned to a thick ebony, almost touching me, that I felt the restlessness grow. I was unsettled, as if I was waiting for something I couldn't put my finger on. It must have been the storm brewing. It was the inexplicable sensation of Evans again. The wind rose, suddenly, swirling the leaves of the silver

birch in the wild space at the far end of the garden. A
downpour was imminent. And sure enough the first drops
started to fall, vertically, bouncing in great splats on the
patio. I frantically raced around the house, which now was
filled with an uncharacteristic inky gloom, to secure the
windows. I noticed I was clammy, my whole body dripping
in sweat and tiny beads of perspiration soaking my upper
lip and brow. I remember wiping the wetness with the
back of my hand as I reached up and pulled down the
sash window in the bedroom that overlooked the garden.

In the half-light, it looked like a pre-historic bird, its
immense wing-span stretched, hovering just feet above
the birches, silhouetted against the sky. And then a violent
rustling as it seemed to swoop downwards and come to a
sudden stop, trapped in the silver leaves of the branches. It
felt primeval and I rolled *Pterodactyl* around in my mouth
with pleasure and with a logic that at that moment made
perfect sense.

It's the wetness I recall now, the cooling deluge of storm-
rain soaking my cotton T-shirt as I raced towards this creature hanging there in the branches, silent and motionless.
This creature whose wings too were sodden and limp. I
could see that the flimsy silk of its wings, the tips like
smoked tallow, had been violently ripped in the fall and
had become detached from the skeletal framework which
reminded me of tributaries of veins. Pathetic somehow,
this loss of flight, this fallen angel.

This was a creature of unspeakable beauty with a fine-
ness of form which was almost unearthly. Not yet fully
mature, you could see the adult that would be in the face
that was finely sculpted, sharp and intense; the skin taut

and translucent, veins showing through the alabaster, the
bloodless lips that looked icy cold, and the eyes, pleading
to be cut free. This mesmerising bird-man had flown into
my garden on a sudden storm one hot August night and
fallen to earth. I felt an instant connection. He gave off an
aura which I sensed even before his arrival.

I must have untangled him from the branches; unhooked
the barbed brambles that had punctured his flesh. I suppose
I might have helped him off with his harness and pack away
his sorry wings. And I would have bathed the scratches on
that face of his – wiped it clean – as my fingertips remained
stained with blood, a juicy rich red-purple, like those fat
ripe blackberries that would soon hang in the lane, just
beyond. I presume I asked him his name, where he came
from, all manner of things as I knew by his accent and his
archaic northern dialect that he wasn't from these parts,
perhaps not even from these times. He simply told me that
his name was Evans. I just have an impression of him leaving, walking down the lane that leads to the sea, trailing his
broken and bedraggled wings from his shoulder, turning
his head, just once, to smile, as he faded into the distance.

Naturally, my husband put it down to the combination of too much sun, heat exhaustion and the virus. The
medical profession reassured him that high temperature,
hallucination and out-of-body experiences followed by total
collapse were typical; recovery was likely to take a long
time. They put the broken branches on the birch down to
the storm that night, the electricity in the air; but no one
could explain the blood on my hands.

Summer passed. When late October came, I ventured
out beyond the five-bar gate and along the lane. The

blackberries had flowered and fruited without my knowledge, save those remaining desiccated few, near which a foulness of blue-black flies buzzed over a heap of dried dung.

Connective Tissue

MAGGIE MORGAN HAS her head in the hole that's been manufactured to accommodate it. She keeps her eyes open and stares down through the dark space at the floor. She's lying flat on her stomach on the black couch in the treatment room.

"How have we been since last time, Maggie?" Jenny asks. "Any pain? Headaches? Tenderness?"

"About the same. No worse. No better," she says.

Her own voice sounds strange to her; distant somehow, as though in a great void. She wonders why it is always necessary to refer to her in the first person plural these days. She can't recall exactly when it first started, though knows it was some medical context or other. *Still mobile are we, Mrs. Morgan? Wearing our distance glasses for driving are we, Mrs. Morgan? Taking our tablets are we, Mrs. Morgan? Opening our bowels regularly are we, Mrs. Morgan?*

She'd like to remind Jenny that she hasn't been a 'we' for almost twenty years, that she is very much an 'I'. Singular. First person. Alone and almost invisible. But she can't somehow bring it up. And she's a lovely girl anyway. Doesn't want to upset her.

"Just going to work down your spine first, Maggie. The usual. Don't mind if I unclasp your bra?"

"Long as your hands aren't cold," she says.

"Warmed them up especially for you. Feel."

She knows Jenny's hands by now: fleshy finger tips, firm, young, know what they're doing. In the snug of the hole, she detaches herself from Jenny the girl and gives herself up to the hands.

There is a thick silence in the room now as Jenny works down Maggie's spine from neck to coccyx, vertebra by vertebra, feeling towards understanding. Maggie is soothed by the process, the pressure on her frame creating a state poised somewhere between pain and pleasure, the warmth and energy radiating though her cold bones.

"There. Done. You can lie down on your back now, Maggie. Have a bit of a breather," Jenny says as she does up Maggie's bra. "Take your time."

Maggie emerges from her cocoon and turns to settle herself as told. Jenny holds the blue blanket to her skin as she shifts round. It feels snug and warm, protective even. She feels comfortable now, easing gently into the Thursday afternoon. From this position, the yellowed skeleton hanging in the corner of the room comes into view along with the clock on the wall signalling that she is already a third of the way through her weekly forty-five-minute session. That £10 has already been used up.

"You're taut as a string, Maggie. Knotted up."

"Mmm. Need to relax. I do try, you know."

"I know you do. Not a criticism . . .Okay. Going to try some organ work, this week. See how we get on with that."

"Organ work?"

"Not just bones, you know. Ligaments. Tendons. Connective tissue," Jenny says.

"Our mysterious inner workings."

"Like join the dots . . .You're going to restore my well-being, then? Just likes it promises on the leaflet," Maggie jokes.

"Do my best. Can't promise, though. Don't do miracles in Mumbles," she says.

"Will it hurt?" Maggie asks.

"Shouldn't do. But everyone's got their own pain threshold. You might feel a little discomfort when you get home. But it'll wear off. Frozen peas will do the trick. Just say, if you want me to stop."

Maggie watches as Jenny lifts her bare, right leg, raises it off the table and pulls it close to her chest. She rotates Maggie's hip gently and then releases the tight grip and asks Maggie to push as hard as she can against her hands, and then let go. Maggie likes the task: the tension in the thigh, the resistance and then the relinquishing, letting the muscles relax, watching her limp leg being placed back on the table. Maggie enjoys the repetition on her left leg. There's comfort in the pattern.

She lies on her left side, then her right, Jenny making sure that the blanket keeps her warm and covered as she works her magic. Jenny presses the soles of Maggie's feet into her hands. She'd always liked having her feet held. She pushes hard into Jenny's palms and then releases, seeing each foot in turn flop back down onto the table.

As Jenny works, Maggie glances at the skeleton. Wonders who the shell once was, now just a scaffold hanging on a hook in the corner of a consulting room in a city suburb:

a collection of bones and joints: femurs, radii, ulnae, tibiae, patellae and a pelvis. She takes a look at the clock again. Almost done.

"You've got a very acrobatic pelvis, you know, Maggie. And your left patella is not exactly where it should be. Nothing major. The accident probably."

"Well, you can't expect to come out unscathed when you've been through what we went through," she says, realising that 'we' is being used in its correct sense for once. He was the last person she'd actually touched; been touched by. "Like you said. It's about more than bones, isn't it?"

"Yeah. Much more than bones," says Jenny.

Maggie lies flat on her back for the last fifteen minutes so that Jenny can continue her healing. She gazes at the intense concentration visible in Jenny's young, unblemished face, trusts her steady, probing fingertips, sure on her sternum as it rises and falls. It's worth it, she thinks. Thirty pounds for forty-five minutes once-a-week is a small price to pay.

"I'm going to leave my hands on your ribcage for a while, to finish off," Jenny says softly. "Breathe slowly. Nice long, easy breaths. In. Out. In. Out. Feel yourself relaxing. Just being. That's it. Good."

After a certain age you can either have good shoes or good feet

T HEY ARE STILL here, my love, one each side of your foot stool, just as they were last night. I suppose in all the kerfuffle they were the last thing we had been thinking about. D'you know, I worried all night about your feet being cold: those lovely feet of yours, lying immobile outside the flimsy, white blanket they had wrapped you in. Strange what you think about; but as I sat in the chair beside your bed, I longed to place these shabby, fur-lined slippers on your tiny feet, stop them from chilling, turning blue.

I suppose I should tidy up and put them away. They look so empty lying there waiting, as though they're ready for you to slip gently back into. I sit pillowed in your winged armchair, put my feet on the velour stool and clutch the slippers in my hands. I finger the fabric, trace the slight mounds that your big toes have moulded in each one: impressions of you. I touch the slight wear on the outside of each rubber heel: that distinctive gait of yours. I caress my cheek with the softness of the uppers; breathe in the smell of you, the passing of time.

You would probably tell me to pull myself together, stop maudlin, get to bed and try to sleep. But I feel too tired to sleep. I'm content here in the snug of your familiar chair, with a feel of your permeating the pores of my skin. It's strange what comes back to you, not the obvious things you think will. How odd to obsess with feet at a time like this. It's probably because you had a thing about feet, one of your best assets, you'd said, and even in your later years you'd always taken a great pride in them. *Some people say that when you reach a certain age, you can either have good shoes or good feet. Well, I'm lucky enough to have both,* I hear you say. And you did. Chiropodists, pedicurists, every fortnight you'd keep those appointments without fail. You even succumbed to the latest craze: those tanks full of toothless Turkish carp that nibbled away at the dead skin of your heels and soles. Ridiculous. Yet it all paid off, for you had the loveliest feet I've ever seen, soft and gentle and unblemished.

I can own up now, nothing to lose: I was always fearful that those feet would walk away from me. Heaven knows, you had enough shoes to satisfy even Imelda Marcos. In our youth, I would imagine you click-clacking away from me to meet a man whose face I could not see; I could just hear the fading echo of your heels along the pavement. Or I'd see you twirling and swirling, your hair curled, a smile on your red-glossed lips, as a man I couldn't recognise, held you in his arms, as you slow-waltzed in silver shoes around a glimmering ballroom. I would love to have been that man; but I had two left feet, you laughed. Though you never walked away, did you? You stayed until the end and I was so happy in our more comfortable, soft-slippered years. So, I will just sit here until I am ready.

And when I think, I'm ready, I take small steps, up the stairs to our bedroom. I turn down the cotton sheets and the waft of Lily of the Valley overwhelms me. Your smell. A smell of long, spring evenings and damp gardens. For the first time since you've been gone, I cry. Crying I don't feel, until the tears pour off my face onto the sheets. I try to settle myself down, but sleep does not come. I feel you there, your long grey hair spread out on the pillow next to me, the rise and fall of your chest at rest, the occasional sigh. Try as I might, I cannot drift off. I put on the bedside light and it is only a hollow depression still left in the pillow of your side of the bed, the book you were reading, cover facing up, spread open at the spine, pages down, ready for you to pick up again from where you'd left off. Your treatment of books, used to niggle me so, but now I wish I'd never said how much it had irritated me – I'm desperate for you to irritate me, to feel alive on the energy of slightly-cross words passing back and fore between us. Do you know, this is the first time I've ever slept alone in this bed? It feels much bigger without you.

And then all I remember is switching off the light and turning on my side, tucking myself into a foetal position, when I hear the sound of music. In my semi-conscious state, I can't work out where it's coming from. The clock says 2pm. We'd never had any trouble with the neighbours before and I wouldn't have thought them to be so insensitive at a time like this.

I pad barefoot across the carpet, led by the strains of the

music. It sounds like a full orchestra. It draws me down the stairs, into the hall, through the kitchen and out into the back garden. There are no lights, no sign of anyone anywhere. There is only the moon, full and milky, casting its marbled glow over the patio and lawn. And it's from our patio that the sound is emanating.

I am thinking, how strange this all is, and wonder if I'm sleep walking, or whether it's perhaps the effects of the hot toddy I've drunk to try and settle myself to sleep. I notice the battered Dansette record player set up on a table, it's red, like the one I had when I was a teenager. It's playing 78s, I can see them stacked under the arm, hear the brief, almost-silence between records as the arm drops the next disc, ready to play, the hum and roll of the spinning vinyl, the distinctive crackle of the stylus in the continuous grooves. It's *Liebestraum*; I recognise it in an instant and I feel the hairs on my forearms respond instinctively.

It's then I smell Lily of the Valley again: cruel the tricks the imagination plays, I think. I've read so much about grief and what it does to the bereaved, though I'd never imagined it would affect me in such a bizarre fashion. This is surely madness. But when I turn towards the birch trees at the far end of the garden, you are there. Everything seems brushed with silver under the moonlight: the leaves of the trees; the dew on the spikes of grass; and your grey hair. From top to toe, you are a vision of loveliness in this peculiar light that is creating such magic in our own ordinary, little garden. Your skin is more translucent than I've even seen it before, stripped of colour, it looks touched with unearthliness; that favourite grey taffeta dress you wore when we were on honeymoon, way back, is transformed into stardust; and to finish this astonishing vision of you, are those shoes, strappy, peep-toed, spangled-silver that you'd love to dance in when we were in our prime.

You don't look happy, or sad, if visions can express emotions, more serene. I'm expecting you to vanish any second as I emerge from what must be a hypnogogic state; but you walk towards me, gliding in silence with the grace of a long-necked swan. I've never seen you looking like this before. It almost takes my breath away.

You place your hand on my arm. It feels icy just as I expected a spirit would; but I'm not at all perplexed. A certain calm comes over me that I haven't felt for weeks. And then you move closer, so we're almost cheek to cheek, though not touching and you whisper in my ear, ask me if I'd like to dance with you, promising that this time, you won't laugh at my two left feet. I hear the words, though there is no sensation of warm breath.

Your offer is irresistible, my love: how I have longed for you since you left me so suddenly, without warning. *Follow me,* you sigh, *I'll lead.* And we start a slow waltz, me managing to keep in 3/4 time as we drift across the grass, in perfect rhythm, perfect synchronicity. I feel light on my feet, like Fred Astaire, I tell you, and you respond in that girlish giggle you always had.

The dancing continues, your head on my shoulder as the 78s play on, some Strauss, some Schubert, a smattering of Tchaikovsky, us gently swaying then, our feet tiring as the last of the records remains spinning and humming on the turntable. Just before dawn. you turn away from me, say that you have to go before the sun is risen. I ask you if that's what spirits have to do; but you just smile and glide back, disappearing into the trees from where you first emerged and I am left with a warm glow of contentment and the sound of the crackle from the Dansette.

I'd like to tell you that I feel I can sleep then, but of course you are not around anymore. None of this is real, you old fool, you silly old man. You've dreamed her up, I tell myself. I read enough to know that grief is a complex state and that combined with a lack of sleep, hallucinatory experiences are quite common. Take it for what it is: a figment of the imagination.

I feel heady with exhaustion, darling, as I mount the stairs and fall into bed. The sun is already risen, but my eyes are heavy and I fall into a deep sleep as soon as my old head touches the pillow. I drift away on the waft of Lily of the Valley. It must be almost lunch when I am roused, with dreams of us dancing, just like the dream I used to have of you dancing with that man whose face I couldn't see, the man I feared you'd always run off with. But now I can see his face clearly as my own. And he is grinning from ear to ear.

I make my way downstairs with a young man's tread, a new spring in my steps. Something seems to have been lifted from me. I feel the tightness relax in my muscles and I breathe out more easily. I walk across the sitting room and have the urge to sit in your chair, to fall into its comfort; let its arms embrace me. It's then I notice that they've gone: your slippers; and in their place is a pair of silver shoes. I recognise them in an instant. They are not new, but worn and familiar, but they have fresh, sappy grass stains on the soles, like the stains that are greening the soles of my bare and aching feet.

Anticlockwise on the Circle Line

G LANCING UP FROM the pavement, I note the time on the old clock tower: ten to eight. Still plenty of time. I take one last look at the original station name still etched proudly on the white façade – *Farringdon and High Holborn*; see the *Parcel Office* sign on the wall. Strange that I'd never noticed that until now. You and I, we, don't seem to be walking in step, or of our own accord; carried on the thrust of the rush hour throng, like dried autumn leaves being swept up off the pavement on Cowcross Street and in through the entrance. Under my left arm, the crudely wrapped parcel you've given me earlier, lies tucked like a jealously guarded secret: I'll deal with it later, when I'm ready; though already I feel its weight pressing against my rib cage.

"Goodbye, Cassie," you say in the way you always have, ever since I have come to know you: using the diminutive, the affectionate. It makes me feel fleetingly young again, a brief scene from an otherwise tragic play in which a middle-aged woman acts out the main role. And then I'm on my own and it's all down to me. I'll have to make decisions.

I descend from street level to the concourse at Level 1, Oyster Card at the ready.

As well as getting me up, helping me to dress in something for the day ahead, you've seen to this for me as well. Always so practical. I could choose to go clockwise, I suppose: it looks about the same distance on the yellow-lined map whichever way you travel – about thirty minutes, thirteen stops, if time and distance matter anymore to this woman in transit.

Barbican . . . Moorgate . . . Liverpool Street . . . Aldgate . . . Tower Hill . . .

I mouth the names like an incantation; but this particular sequence does not appeal, not this morning. I feel accosted here in this vast space where the whole of London seems to be on the move, closing in: the young, with their walking shoes and their bags slung across their shoulders, earplugs shutting out the world, sure of where they're going. I wipe the sweat from the back of my neck, put on my dark glasses, trying to shield my eyes from the sickly glare of the fluorescent strip lights, close my ears to the incessant clank of the trains one level below and the interminable automated safety announcements about unattended luggage. One of those headaches has already started. There's a taste of metal on my tongue. I clutch the parcel ever-closer to my breast.

Farringdon . . . King's Cross . . . Euston Square . . . Great Portland Street . . . Baker Street . . .

Something from deep within urges me to choose anti-clockwise to St. James's Park. I push on through the crush, descending to Level 2 for the trains, looking for the one that will take me in the direction that has called to me. Via Edgware Road flashes up on the panel. Next train expected in 2 minutes. I feel invisible among all these commuters, detached, even from myself. *I* am becoming *she,* a spectator outside my own body, an omniscient spirit floating in a world I no longer seem to inhabit. A woman going somewhere on an autumn morning, beneath the streets of London, journeying through the tunnels where there seems no context. I step though the sliding doors and heave my body onto a vacant seat as we pull out of the station.

Though it's wedged to capacity, there's an unearthly silence in the car, though they're looking in my direction, these tallow-faced passengers: ghostly stares, trying to avoid my eyes. It's the parcel they're drawn to; the warnings, I expect. And this woman, they perhaps suspect. Everyone is suspected of something these days. I snuggle the present close to me, fearful of ever losing it.

I am gulped into tunnels of blackness, into the heat and griminess of this subterranean world. It feels timeless, another universe almost. Though there's the smoothness of electric modernity, there comes from out of nowhere, a whiff of the past, a judder and jolt, a sense of steam, dust and decay. I recall from somewhere that this line was first built to freight dead meat to the terminus at West Smithfield Street. I wonder whether my stony-faced travelling companions can smell it too; that distinctive sweet smell of rotting flesh that I'm breathing in. And with it comes memory.

I catch a glimpse of my reflection in the smeared window of the carriage. Is that woman with the greying hair really me? I switch my gaze to the map above: Edgeware Road . . . Paddington. I'm voicing the syllables out loud. I savour the taste of them rolling around the mouth's chamber. The expressions of the passengers wedged in this space with me suggest that perhaps I am focusing too intently on the yellow line and the twenty-seven stations that are plotted out neatly in diagrammatic form. But I continue what I'm doing, taking note, ticking them off mentally, one by one. Perhaps I won't alight at St. James Park at all; perhaps I'll just stay on board for the twenty-seven stations, just for the sheer hell of it. Perhaps I'll sit in my seat in the midst of this anonymity and simply keep going around and around in a never-ending continuous loop for ever and ever, here in this strange black underground. A woman with an unusual parcel, not quite knowing where she is travelling to, where the end stop might be.

They can't stop eyeing my present. Suspicious creatures. From time to time they shift their gaze from their kindles to my nebulous form, where your gift, my darling, lies resting snug in my spreading lap. I can't blame them, I suppose; for it's a peculiar package: the shape, the soft, almost fur-like fabric, the way it's secured with white string, looped into six neat sections and secured with a reef knot. They've probably never seen anything like it in all of their young lives. But I have. I've seen a meat-bag like this before, way back in childhood.

There's Dad in our butcher's shop, wrapping joints and long-forgotten cuts of slow-cooking flesh, stewing steak, shin, skirt, brisket. Rust-red liver, like a redundant afterbirth, flops on white greaseproof, the blood trickling through his fingers, before he tucks the folded greaseproof inside old newspapers and slips the wrapped meat into the plastic wallets inside the furry parcel. The sickly-sweet smell is stronger now, pervading my nostrils, filling the carriage with its stench; but these commuters don't seem to notice, they just keep staring and then averting their gaze when their eyes meet mine.

Bayswater . . . Notting Hill Gate . . . High Street Kensington . . .

I will have to make my mind up soon, though decisions are so hard to make at my time of life, amid the rattling clutter of my mind that these fellow travellers cannot hear, these characters with non-speaking parts in my mid-life drama beneath the streets of London. I see them lower their heads and shift back to their iPhones, their tablets, as I caress the velvety parcel with my ageing hands. They will remain blind and deaf to the flood of menstruation as I grieve for my young uterus, fresh and fertile.

It is tenseless and senseless down here in this place where the dark creeps around the carriage like a hot musty blanket. I feel primeval now as I start to notch the passing of time. I am fifty. If my life had run its natural course, as it perhaps had been mapped out, then I would have bled through three hundred and twenty-four menstrual cycles since that final one; twelve for very one of the twenty-seven stations on this Circle route I'm passing through. I'm aware my thinking is not as it should be; but feel powerless to alter its course. I will go with the flow, like this momentous journey I am making on my own, with just my precious parcel.

Gloucester Road . . . South Kensington . . . Sloane Square . . .

Almost there. Just two more stops. And now inside the carriage it's nauseous in that overly-hot London way. The carriage lights are stark and yellow-white, and the probing stares and silence from the eyes that surround me pierce me like that surgeon's scalpel. That scalpel that stole my future before I ever met you, my serious and sensitive soul-searcher who I have left abandoned in the station back at Farringdon. I close my eyes before we pull into Victoria.

I drift in and out of semi-consciousness, lulled by the monotony of the engine. I feel myself being sucked ever more backwards, rooting into the past. I need to sleep, to shut it all out; but peace does not come easily these days, especially now with the package in tow. Restless whispers and murmurings are melding into a cacophony which is splitting my head, as I try to doze to the accompaniment of the rhythm of the train on the track. But demons are lurking here in these caverns:

I'm sorry, it's not good news – but at least we've got it early and at least you had your children young.

You look so well, can't believe something so horrible is going on inside . . . thank God it isn't your arm!

You'll be no good to anybody . . . no-one will ever want you now. You're doomed to stay with me for ever and ever and ever and ever . . .

And then I'm back in the ward from the antiseptic theatre with the sharp lights like these on this train and I wake to white wimples and the soft-dimpled innocence and gentle Irish lilts of the nuns at my bedside as they tong the miles of brown-blooded gauze from the secret tunnels between my parted thighs and pile the bandages to form white mountains in shimmering stainless steel dishes, shaped like kidneys. They daub the raw gash in my belly with iodine as I ramble with the morphine and cry for the womb they have taken away. For I never had chance to say goodbye and I don't know where they have put it, this sacred part of me. And they have cut me from my past and from my future.

And later, much later, the fortune teller says:

Have you lost a baby? There should have been a third baby?

I come to and wonder whether the passengers can hear my sobs. But of course they can't for my wails are lodged deep inside, silently festering. But you, who I have left to wait and wonder back at Farringdon, must have been looking for my womb all this time, ever since we met. It is so like you to do something like that for me, without even telling me. And you have found it, for today when you took me as far as you could, and left me at the station, you handed me this present which I'm clinging on to. For it is part of me. It contains my lost hope. I know it does. You have given me back my womb and with it the chance of a child that might one day, just be.

. . . St. James Park . . .

But I decide against it. I'm not ready yet so I carry on anticlockwise.

. . . Westminster . . . Embankment . . . Temple . . . Black-friars . . .

I continue to look at my route on the map, absorbed in its never-endingness. I lose track of the stations, time and direction seem to be disappear and find myself already back in Farringdon. I check my watch: it's only fifty-five minutes since I set out. One complete cycle; but I'm nowhere near ready yet. I'm hungry for oblivion to feed on the dank contextless space for a little while longer, however long a little while is, looping through the dizziness of my personal Hades, on my lonely journey through the underworld, far beneath the madness of twenty-first century London.

And now it surely it must be evening already. An arcane chorus as though from a Greek Tragedy sweeps into the carriage soundlessly on a sheet of icy cold air that cuts through me to the bone and gristle. They are swathed identically in funereal, black taffeta or silk, I cannot tell, but with complexions of alabaster. They, like me, find them-selves here, in this sunken world of otherness, endlessly circling this infinite track.

But I am spent and I want to go home. I know you will be there already; waiting. Asking no questions, demanding no explanations. You simply know I will return when I am ready. I rise from my seat, shaking slightly, and abandon my precious parcel – my gift from you, alive with possibility. I am done with it now. I exit the carriage without a backward glance. If I had, I might have noticed the seep of fresh blood on the fabric of my seat which would leave an indelible carmine stain.

Words

I LOVE WORDS. Always have. Words are my job – I'm a teacher of linguistics. When I was young and my name was Evelyn Foster, I would list the words I loved most in a feint-lined pocket notebook with a red cover. Diligently, I would add new words to the list as they thrilled me with their sound – usually on a weekly basis: neatly; in block capitals; word on the left and the reason why I liked them on the right. It looked something like this:

Words I like most by Evelyn Foster aged 11.

LULLABY	I like the gentle sound. I think it's the l. It is a sleepy word.
SIGH	This is a soft word. It hardly makes a sound.
GOSSAMER	We had this word in a poem at school, I don't remember what it means but it sounds light and weightless. The m is a nice sound, airless, tickles the lips.
MELLIFLUOUS	We had this in a poem by John Keats – it was in a phrase the mellifluous haunt of flies of summer eves and Mr. Ware

told us that the words actually *sounded* like the noise the flies make – I can't remember the word he used, on a mat or something, but it was very clever.

This, I suppose, was the time I began to realise that the sounds of words could help re-enforce meaning, or semantics, as they say in our profession. Or perhaps I should say as *I* say in *my* profession. Though I've tended not to say much these last few years that uses the personal or possessive pronoun. Strange for someone in my line of work who loves words so much.

I still write though, as I used to, in a little spiral-bound exercise book which I squirrel away in my bedside drawer. I'm still a stickler for recording words and phrases that are memorable, that strike me for some reason or other. I use the same basic template; word or phrase or utterance (not sentence – we are talking here, spoken not written language) on the left and a brief description of my personal response on the right. It looks something like this:

Memorable words & phrases by Evelyn Francis* age 51 (I forgot, this book has a black cover.)

CLAP TRAP Memorable. One syllable. Punchy. Repetition of phonetic /aep/

---

* sometimes I think that my mother might have been right with her little rhyme:
Change the name and not the letter
Change for worse and not for better

FLAPPING YOUR LIPS	Hate this. Images of birds. When accompanied by hand action, in close up, it is terrifying.
SHUT THE FUCK UP	Menacing. Keeps repeating in my head. Anglo-Saxon monosyllabic word.
KEEP YOUR GOB SHUT AND YOUR LEGS OPEN	Use of the declarative – always so many commands.
WHO NEEDS A DEGREE WHEN THERE'S THE UNIVERSITY OF LIFE?	Yes, the eternal chip on the shoulder.
A GOOD KICKING	Implies repeated action, a series of kicks, becomes a collective noun.
A PUNCH IN THE GOB	Onomatopoeic and monosyllabic.
ON AND ON	Hypnotic chain of lexis . . . .
AND ON AND ON	how long? My God, how long?

I trust you get the gist. My recorded writing tends to be less regimented and more *ad hoc,* as they say. I write as and when an event occurs – sometimes daily, sometimes weekly. Sometimes I'll go for a few weeks without the need to record. But this is most unusual. I find this way I can create more immediacy and attempt to make more sense of things.

If someone somewhere, an outsider, were to analyse these books, I think it would be relatively simple to draw some conclusions linguistically. I often recast my professional eye – expert and objective – over my childhood lists of vocabulary. Literary, multi-syllabic, often Latinate, sometimes poetic. I then analyse the vocabulary I am immersed in forty years on. Non-literary, colloquial, vernacular, often clichéd platitudes and collocations, simple lexis, mostly single syllables, use of onomatopoeia (that was the word I couldn't recall in childhood but I know it know) predominant use of Anglo-Saxon lexis especially for action words, doing words, verbs such as punch, kick, slap, split.

I would assume the analyst would pose the question, *What does this language tell us about the speaker's gender? Ethnicity? Social class? Attitudes and Values?* I would be able to say quite a lot, I feel, on that subject about these people. I would go so far as to say I would be able to write up a substantial report based on my suppositions and conclusions. I would be able to draw a lot of inferences about the speaker – on paper at least. I might even form opinions, judgments, pointers for action, the range of desirable outcomes that objective professionals make. For I have to keep telling myself, I am, after all, a professional.

I have friends who are high functioning alcoholics: I'm in good company, and I believe I still function like the best of them, at least I have done until now. No-one outside these four walls would ever know – not even my Mother and Father. To them I'm still their little girl who has everything, a good-looking husband with his own business, my own profession, three beautiful children, two granddaughters, a home in the country, the Labrador dog, the pewter Aga. I was the first person they knew to have a built-in waste-disposer and a self-cleaning oven. What would they think if they'd known I'd sold my soul for a

Mercedes Benz? *Domestic violence is no respecter of income, you know*, I feel like screaming, *or social class*. But of course, I don't. I am dumb to tell them. My voice is no longer even a whisper. But I have my black book.

Back in the late seventies when I was in my twenties, there was a song by Billy Joel called, 'But She's Always a Woman to Me' that he'd keyed into. He had a terrible voice but he'd always sing it to me.

So perhaps there was a time when there was love. But there was always the ugly spectre of fear and insecurity and I mistook power and control for love. And already by the early eighties, by the time we'd had our third fitted kitchen put in, he was telling me quite rationally how they'd never find my body. I remember distinctly as it was the brand spanking-new kitchen appliances that acted as the catalyst for what he deemed very creative thinking:

the waste disposer	This was cutting edge and plumbed into the sink. It enabled food waste – bones, vegetable skins, fats – to be stuffed into the large aperture in the sink with a plunger and then ground down with the blade mechanisms in the steel body of the machine. The residue would simply drain away with the water without trace . . .
the self-cleaning oven	This was a fan-assisted double-oven with the great advantage of no cleaning. You simply set the dial to self-clean and the oven

would heat to the intensity of an
inferno. Any food residue that
was in the oven would be burnt
to cinders. All that would remain
was a small heap of fine white dust
which could be wiped away in a
simple flick with a damp cloth . . .

His other *wheeze,* as he used to call it, to dispose of
me, was just not worth bothering about after the kitchen
appliances had been installed. Boring and predictable for
someone to accidentally fall off a narrow cliff path when
out for a walk with the husband and the dog, wasn't it? I
have to say, I agreed with him. It was always best to agree.

Recently, my daughter had a waste disposer and a
fan-assisted oven installed in her swish house in Barnes.
Co-incidentally they are *Neff* too and when I heard the
grinding of the motor and the whirring of the fan over
the Christmas period, I felt suddenly sick and shut myself
in her downstairs cloakroom, retching violently into the
lavatory. I felt outside myself in a way I've never felt before,
a spectator observing a play. Perhaps it was the time of
year that brought about a feeling of not being myself at all.

She asked me to stay on a while into the New Year. Why
not? I thought, I didn't have to be back in school until the
12th January. So *he* went home. People depended on him,
he said, the world didn't stop turning in business like it
did in education. And he gave me one of those looks, the
look with the muscle twitch under the left eye. I didn't say
anything. But I stayed.

It was when I went to the bedroom that I really started

to feel peculiar – cold and clammy, vibrations running down my legs and in my stomach. It was almost as though a big black bird with enormous wings was flapping inside my body, beating my skin from the inside out. I tried to take deep breaths the way I had through the years when I felt I was losing control, before I could get to my little black book. But it wasn't working. My breath was coming in spasms and I felt dizzy. There was a metallic taste in my mouth, the way I'd have before my periods when I was younger. I needed my book. Record words. Make calm out of the chaos that was playing out before me in my daughter's bedroom with floor-to-ceiling mirrors on the wardrobe doors.

And that's when I saw her, looking at me from the mirror. She was waving at me, her hands gesturing me towards the glass. She was trying to say something, but the sound was muffled, indistinct. Instinctively, I drew towards her. I recognised her, though she'd changed so much in the intervening years. The dark curly hair was long gone, replaced with what some might call hair like pepper and salt. The eyes were somehow sadder and looking into them brought about an almost convulsive sob, primitive and animal; a lone sob in a frightening world. I thought of those eyes as they'd been, alive with anticipation and enquiry. The eyes of the girl who was always smiling. The girl who never stopped talking.

I sat on the edge of the bed and stretched out my hands, fingertip to fingertip with the girl in the glass. She struggled to talk, but she persisted in trying. Face to face we were then, close-up, and I could see, and smell, adhesive. It was caked along her lips, congealed in globules at the corners of her mouth. I knew it was *Bostik* at once, for when my daughter was a tiny girl, and I'd been cleaning out drawers, she'd put a tube of it in her mouth and chewed. She'd bitten through the tube and the glue had stuck fast. In terror, I'd taken her to A & E. It was the fear, always the fear. They'd take my children away. The Social Workers. I was an unfit parent. He'd never let me have my kids. What good would I be to anyone without him? I'd go crawling back. What was I without him? I would be nothing. It must have been at that *Bostik* moment that I began losing my voice.

I dipped gently into the reflection. With my index finger, I began picking the glue away from her top lip with my nail. I delved into both corners and scraped a little harder. I could feel the warmth of her breath and at the same time, could feel an itching sensation in my own mouth. I worked on, prizing her lips wider to reveal the teeth, the tongue, allowing the hidden mechanics of the mouth freedom. Her lips parted and the sounds she uttered became audible. The larynx, the vocal chords, the mouth's inner chamber all began to work together. *Where did you go?* she shouted, *where did you go?*

Her anger was disconcerting, but perfectly justified, I reasoned. I'd let myself down, perhaps all women down, for reasons only I would ever know. For an intelligent woman I'd made some very unwise decisions in my fifty-one years. I stood up and stared full-on at the girl in the mirror. *I'm still here,* I whispered and then a little louder, *I'm still here.* She said nothing but smiled and gave me the thumbs-up. I still couldn't find my book, but I wasn't in a state about it at all. I grabbed one of the grandchildren's magic markers, a big fat red one and scrawled over the clear glass mirror in upper-case I'M STILL HERE AND I'VE FOUND MY VOICE !!!! with not one, but four exclamation marks which professionally, I'd normally hate for two reasons. Firstly, the over-zealous use of this punctuation device and secondly, because it's simply such bad grammar to use four rather than one. They tell me this ink is indelible; it'll be a bugger for my daughter to get rid of. But the girl in the mirror disappeared as soon as I began to write, turning her head just once to check on me and smile as she walked into the distance beyond the back of the fitted wardrobes.

Crow

I T'S COMING UP to 26th April. I'm counting the days. There's a black-penned circle around the date in my diary and a note: Katy's twelve-week scan. Not that I need reminding. Not anymore. I seem to live each new day of my daughter's pregnancies with her and I've been sharing her unease for weeks. I wish I could be nearer to her at times like this; my grown-up baby at one end of the M4 and me, the other.

The physical distance between us seems too much at the moment so I calculate the numbers in time rather than miles. It's only 3 hours 20 minutes if I really need to get my foot down between Gower and Fulham. My bag is always at the ready; on constant stand-by, just like me. Though I suppose it's natural for a mother to be anxious when her daughter is expecting yet another baby: a baby that will never materialise into a grandchild that can be touched, and held and kissed. It will probably be absorbed for no earthly-known reason, like all the others, into a vile worm-hole where God is dividing the universe by zero.

It's just before dusk when I take the call in bed. And I'm scared. It must be that she hasn't made the twelve-week scan again. Ectopic. It must be. I know in an instant by the symptoms: there's pain in her shoulder and spotting. I call it mother's instinct; she calls it catastrophising. Just let me know if there's any change, I say, don't take any risks. Get down the Chelsea and Westminster Hospital, just as a precaution. She promises she will. I need to be there, but I can't. She's alright she says, she has her husband, Tom, and she's actually not a baby anymore, so why don't I just go to bed and try to get some sleep. I say, I'll do as I'm told and try.

I hear it before I see it: rapping at the window. Insistent. Incessant. Still heavy from dreams and sleep, I presume it is unseasonal hail nailing against the glass that has shocked me into the day: light is peeking through the gap between the natural linen curtains. It's just enough to see its shadow.

At first it is with wings extended, a mass of fluted symmetrical darkness; black on white, and the silhouette of its beak, bobbing back and fore, hammering as if demanding admittance. And then I hear the flap of its wings against the bottom pane as it folds them into itself and perches motionless on the sill.

My heart is palpitating and my body motionless too, in synchrony with this creature of the dawn that is disturbing more than my sleep. I had hoped it would all be well this time; that things would have panned out. But I feel that Crow knows something we mere mortals don't know yet. I have to get it away, sweep away this first occurrence. I don't want to know what it means. I pad from the bed and draw back the curtains to reveal all its sombre ugliness: Crow.

It fixes me through the glass with its jet-beaded eyes as if it recognises my face from another time, another place. I avert my gaze; shift it down its plump body. Beneath the lower frame, where I've pushed up the weighted sash up slightly to let some air through the late spring night, its spiky twig legs and claws are touchable. In stark close-up, I realise that its body isn't crow-black at all; but gives off a green and purple sheen that I've only even seen before in petrol under sunlight. Its bill moves slightly, almost quizzically, as if asking me to heed what it's trying to tell me. It's solitary. I don't like the number one. I pull down the sash and lock the clasp, knowing that it will be stifling in this bedroom for the next few nights.

Crow's presence seems to confirm my worst fears though of course I don't confide in my daughter when she calls, don't tell her about the early-morning visitor, the messenger of death. But she berates me anyway for the negativity she can sense in my voice on the phone, even though I'm trying my hardest to conceal it. She's fine she tells me: *don't worry, keep positive*. She understands that I can't be there all the time and there's no need to go on another guilt-trip.

But I am there, all the next night. My dreams tell me what is playing out in SW6 from two-hundred miles west. Crow is roosting in the birches at the far end of my garden. I can see it silvered by the crescent moon. I am covering my ears to the cacophony of its calls which are echoing through the still night: short and long vowel caws and koo-aws and eh-aws that are urgent and unsettling. *Listen to me*, it's saying, *you cannot be deaf to my message*. I take my palms away from my ears and begin to translate its peculiar tongue into my language, rationally, that way you can only do in dreams. *I am a scavenger*, it mocks; *I steal eggs from other birds' nests. I chew on carrion of new born lambs. I peck eye-sockets of the still warm, stillborn. I crack wombs like I crack nuts, my beak sucks on the embryos of women's hopes.*

I wake trembling to the ratting at the window again. This time, I try to ignore it, tuck my head under the duvet and pray that it will go away.

A couple of beeps, a text coming though: Mum – am in C & W hospital waiting 2 c Dr. Ring u in the morning. Luv Katy x. sent 5.30 a.m.

I ring her back immediately. She still has hope for this little one, she says. She feels it in her bones. There are other feelings making my bones ache. Which will it be? I think; and again, struggle to keep these things to myself, let the situation unravel without interference. *Listen, Mum*, she says, *my HCG levels are over 25,000 so I'm still pregnant. It could be an appendicitis or gastroenteritis. Let's wait for the scan before we write this baby off. It's a numbers game*, she says, *and the odds are still with me.* I'm no fool with statistics by now and know she's not telling me that her levels are at the lowest point on the scale.

A numbers game, she's said. Yes, I think. Numbers. The number three. There will be a third time for Crow before this latest crisis comes to yet another withering and premature ending. I do not trust my daughter's bones anymore: those bones that choose not to snap under the weight of successive disappointment. Like the woman in the moon, she keeps smiling in the midst of her own lunacy as I descend into bedlam with her.

And the moon is ripe on this the third night as I try to sleep, taut with anticipation of Crow at dawn and the ominous news from my baby who thinks she is not a baby anymore

The dream begins with a slow monotonous wing-beat. I can sense a chill gnawing my cheeks, as the flapping displaces the cold night air as Crow approaches me. It is bathed in the sickly glare of the full moon which wears a leer on its face to match Crow's. Crow is enlarging as I watch, its distorted belly engorging, swelling through its plumage. It is so close I fear that its claws will part my hair, scratch my scalp, but it comes near enough only for me to see its feathery nostrils and feel the exhalation of its warm breath on the tip of my nose. And then it is gone to leave me start awake and shivering.

I vow I will stay on high-alert; scare off its arrival with the power of my intention instead of the shimmer and clatter of saucepans. Even though it is some place other in the deep of night, it will surely know I am thinking about it, anticipating. It's that kind of bird. Perhaps if I can stop it coming with the power of my thought, then I can stop what will happen as a consequence.

As dawn breaks, its beak is drumming outside with unbearable intensity. I will front up, I think, so I rip open the curtains to reveal myself as unafraid on the other side of the window. I will try to protect my offspring and her germ of an offspring from this life-grabber; for that's all I can do. I don't avert my gaze this time and for a second Crow freezes, tilts its head to the side as if asking me a question. Its eyes connect and its expression seems to change. And then it is gone into the April morning that is about to break.

Mad with love, I push up the sash as far as it will go. There is nothing between us now. I feel I could screech if only I'd let myself, release the unearthly sounds that have been stuck inside my head for years; but instinct holds me back. Instead, a quiet strength fills me and I inhale slowly, hold my breath for as long as I can, and then exhale with such force that I'm sure my daughter will feel the warm air on her cheek in Chelsea.

My mobile alerts me to another text. I reach for the phone in the murk. So it has come: Mum – have been for emergency scan. Heartbeat heard. Ring me back if you're awake. Pic attached. Luv Katy x. Sent 5.30 a.m.

On the screen a white bean of life free-floats in a big black bubble.

It is What it Is

E ARLIER I'D FOUND myself suggesting that we walk to where the ruins of the Holiday Inn stood behind the spiked perimeter fence. A strange thing to do on a Christmas Day morning, I know, but nevertheless she'd agreed without the need for any persuasion. I don't know what my real motivation was; that subconscious stirring in the mind. Perhaps it was something other than what came from my lips. *I'd like to take some new pictures for my website.*

This was not a first for her: thirty-three years ago she'd been here to south-east Florida with the man she'd been married to before me. They'd stayed at the Holiday Inn Oceanside when its distinctive green logo must have been fresh and promised so much, lighting up the façade of the low-rise hotel that fronted the Atlantic and backed on to South Oceanside Drive. I'd seen her face freeze when we passed it as we drove to our condo. I was struck by her sudden silence at the sight of it, a solitary and desolate wreck in the midst of this otherwise newly developed shore, lined with the wall to wall gleam and shine of high-rise condominiums.

"What are we like?" she joked as I packed up my camera equipment. "Sure you want to do this on Christmas Day?"

"Me? Can you?"

"Course. Told you before, I had a shit time there – but I want to see what's happened to it."

"Don't tell your kids. Stir it all up."

"Promise," she said. "They'd think I'd finally lost the plot."

Apart from the sanderlings and brown pelicans, we were the only souls on the beach as we set southwards along the strand line at that unearthly hour. It was less than a mile but under leaden skies, dripping with humidity and a hot south-easter that hit us headlong, the trudge was sapping. The shore break shelved steeply and the sand shifted beneath our feet; a hard grind on calves and ankles puffed with heat.

We didn't speak much. I'd put that down to the effort we needed to front the eerie wind, nor did we clasp hands as we usually did as my back pack, laden with the paraphernalia of camera equipment, was cutting into my sunburned shoulders. And anyway, each of us was holding our newly-purchased flip-flops, taking care not to get doused with the unpredictable surge of waves which seemed to swell out of nowhere.

She held her head down and fixed her eyes on the seaweed and shells that frilled the damp sand. I knew what she was looking for – the perfect sand dollar. So far she'd found only fragments of this beautiful bleached sea urchin – two points of the five-pointed star, a couple of holes. But like a four-leaf clover, it was unlikely that she'd ever find the complete thing. Not that she'd stop searching.

It was the legend that captivated her: one side of the flat, desiccated treasure to do with Christmas and light, the other to do with Easter, crucifixion and resurrection. As for me, I didn't buy into myth and folk lore – or religion for that matter. And as for Christmas, I hated it. That's why we were here. But as I watched her walk, and read her expression, I wondered if it were ever possible to evade what Christmas carried with it.

If I am honest, I was afraid then. Afraid of what she was thinking, about her past, about him, about being here. Though he had not been a part of her life for over twenty years, I felt he'd never gone away, that his presence was always with us. I'd gone to live in the very same village that she'd lived in with him. I'd come to the other side of the Atlantic to the very same stretch of shore she'd shared with him. And now I'd invited him in again to join us on Christmas Day.

"My God," she uttered as we approached the hotel.

A cloud of black vultures circled at low altitude directly overhead the carcass of the hotel. Another few perched motionless on rotting fence stumps. I said nothing; but felt a shiver creep over my forearms.

"Sniffing out the ghosts of the past," I replied. "Gorging on carrion and rottenness."

I felt an uncomfortable churning in my stomach with the realisation that I, like those hook-billed marauders with their grasping talons, was voracious at the thought of yesterday's gristle.

"Don't joke," she admonished, "they're just here, nowhere else."

We watched as the black-clothed tearers swooped and

scavenged for fish, or abandoned eggs, or something else that was decaying. I'd expected that raptors would screech and squawk; but all was still. The gulls had made themselves absent, and there was just a hollow emptiness in the air as the vultures glided in a large sooty group, the silence broken only by the flap of their enormous wingspan in brief bursts.

"Let's have a snoop around," she said, trying to lift the mood.

I took out my Canon as we picked our way through the shingle, over the fine sand and into the dunes where a wire fence had, at one time, been erected around the forlorn building. I selected the right lens and set the time exposure to automatic. I would just shoot. Gone were the days when you had to be choosy, when film was expensive. I could sort and sift later. I focused and clicked on the signs which had fallen off their fastenings – FENSE TO RENT; VIOLATORS WILL BE PROSECUTED – as we gawped through the torn and yawning gaps in the rusting mesh.

"I can't believe this," she said as she walked away from where I was down on one knee, trying to get an interesting angle of vision on the twin towers of the roof. The green tin had been ripped off in parts and was beating repetitively.

"It must have been terrifying," she added.

I assumed she was talking about hurricane Jeanne that had unleashed its fury as it hit shore directly here in Hutchinson Island, in September, 2004. We'd read about the winds that wheezed like accordions, the sand that had been swept and scoured off the ocean floor and deposited itself three-feet thick in the buildings along this stretch. It had been a time of obliterated landscapes and this hotel had been suffocated and its heart ripped out.

"Look!" she shrieked, "the restaurant I was telling you about, the one in my holiday snaps."

She'd told me wistfully about the floor-to-ceiling panoramic glass windows of the restaurant in this little courtyard with the ochre and Umbrian shades of crazy paving, once so proudly '70s, now so pathetically out of place. She'd told me how the spray from the waves would sometimes splash against the panes that December, not normally the month for tropical storms. I looked at the sorry expanse in front of me, boarded up, ASAP daubed in bold capitals in black paint. I imagined her young self, sitting at the table behind the cheap wood, a glass in her hand, laughing with him, without me. I clicked quickly on the ASAP. I presumed it referred to the local pressure to get this eyesore developed as soon as possible, and not leave it languishing here, a dying legacy to the power of Nature. Everywhere else had re-invented itself, *moved on*, as they say, determined to rebuild and overcome adversity. All but the Holiday Inn.

"I've never seen your holiday snaps. Never," I said.

"Haven't you? Sorry . . .thought you had. There's none of me anyway – he never took any of me, or us together so don't worry. More concerned with the size of the swell and the shape of the waves. That's why we came. Too cold in December for surfing in the UK back then. Didn't have the wetsuits they have these days. Thought he could just wear a summer suit or even his baggies here. Planned to stay in for hours . . . Anyway, it's much smaller than I remember," she added.

She was referring to the pool, which was now covered over with chip board, lifting at the rims to reveal the rubbish – palm fronds, dune grasses – floating on the surface of the fetid water.

"To think I swam in there once with the kids in their little orange arm bands. And sat on plastic white loungers, just there, out of the wind. It was so cold."

Her eyes were scanning the pool area, the shallow and deep end markings, and the timber steps that led into the main body of the hotel. I wondered if she was seeing it in colour snaps or black and white, or in a home movie reel that stuttered through, frame by frame: her face, the children swimming, his face looking on, smiling, all soft hues and gentle tints, the lens smeared with Vaseline. I had a brief thought about Photoshopping him out of the imagined scene and superimposing an image of my young self. I closed down the mental images quickly and reverted to my mission: lines and curves – the vertical pillars, the sharp edges of the steps. It seemed it was all hard lines, not much softness to focus on.

"Didn't realise it was cold when you came before. Thought it would have been warm . . . like now?" I asked.

"Cold? It was bone cold. They said it was the coldest winter in living memory, so bitter that the citrus crops died. Scuppered his plans for spending days on his board."

She walked along the perimeter of the fence then, her bare feet carefully negotiating the Spanish bayonets, purslane and railroad vine that was creeping its way landward. It was tangling itself into knots as it crept towards the little courtyard as if it wanted to choke it to death, devour it as if it had never been. I caught her face in profile, her hair blowing in the wind as she turned her back to me, standing, staring at the façade of the hotel. She hated having her picture taken. Like the Seminole Indians who once lived in these parts, she perhaps feared the camera would capture her soul.

Deep down, I wanted to interrogate her: shuck her barnacled shell, for her to tell me what it was like being married to him. But she remained sealed. Watertight. I plodded on with the task in hand. At least I took comfort in the fact that I could take the occasional good photograph. She'd even complemented me on my distinctive eye, my instinctive feel for composition. *I think your pictures tell stories,* she'd told me.

And there were stories here in front of me, stories waiting to be told. FUCK YOU and SEX had been aero-sprayed across the sand-coloured concrete walls, over the salt-smeared windows. Some windows had been smashed, distinctive bulls-eye holes at their centres, cracks radiating out like desperate outstretched arms. One window had been wrenched open so you could see the flimsy shreds of curtain billowing in the distraught air. There was graffiti on the inside pane, squatters I expect; but I was unable to decipher the mirror writing, understand the secret messages they'd left behind.

She came towards me, perplexed.

"I've been trying to work out which room we stayed in, but I can't remember. I thought it was a sea-facing room with a balcony but look, they're just Juliettes . . . and there was sun . . . I remember sun in the early evenings. So it couldn't have been ocean-facing – the sea faces east."

She was talking non-stop then, trying to make sense of things.

"It's that one," she said pointing up, "the one on the end with the open window. Look! You can see right through to the window on the far side of the room that overlooks the Intra-Coastal Waterway, the west that gets the late afternoon sun."

I took more photographs as she talked, the disc must have been almost full.

"Yes, that's definitely the one," she said, lost in time. "I've got a snap of Ben when he was four standing right in front of that window, dressed in his Incredible Hulk matching vest and pants, the ones he'd had from Santa that morning. And Laura when she was five, sitting smiling in an armchair, her brand-new red and white gingham all-American frock lit by the pink glow of sunset, Cat in the Hat, stretched proudly on her lap."

I noticed, for once, what could have been tears in her eyes. She looked towards me, into me.

"See, there were some good times," I said.

"With the kids there were," she said.

"But you *must* have had some good times – you and him. It can't have been all bad."

She said nothing. It was the longest pause I have ever known.

"No. No good times. Eighteen years of shit."

And it was at that instant I believed her. I was satisfied with her truth. It would have been one of those acclaimed camera-stills that said it all. We turned our backs on the destruction behind and she returned to joke-mode.

"Seems there've been a few hurricanes that have come

through here," she quipped as we started the long trek back to the condo. My equipment put away by then, and the wind pressing on the small of my back, my load felt lighter.

"Get any good shots d'you think?" she asked with genuine interest, her face full of earnest.

"Some, I hope," I said.

"Well, let's have a look, then," she instructed. "We'll find somewhere to sit down."

We squeaked on for a little longer through the soft sand to where a beautiful bleached boardwalk ran on to the beach, its white rope hand rails bright in the sunshine that was forging through the fast moving cumulus clouds. A peep of cyan was visible. It looked promising. We sat on the timber steps and she leaned in to my shoulder as I took the camera out of the bag and set the dial to VIEW.

"Have a look," I said, "see what you think."

Image by image, she scrutinised every shot. Her face was calm. I thought she looked fleetingly young again, younger somehow than she had earlier that morning, the sun gleaming on the hair that she was finally allowing to go grey, lighting up the deep crows' feet at the corners of her eyes. *No point fighting it,* she'd told me. *It is what it is.*

"With a bit of work, I could have a couple that will do for the website," I said, as she carried on the slide show.

"Don't like airbrushing," she said. "You can't Photoshop the truth."

And with the tip of her index finger, one by one, she deleted every shot.

Controlled Explosions

Paul has his left foot pressed down hard on the clutch of the Mitsubishi.

"You alright to drive?" asks Dave, seated with him upfront.

"It's not me. It's this heap of shit," says Paul. "It's slipping again."

"I wasn't accusing you – and I can smell it now – I just wondered how you were. You know, with Christmas on top of things," says Dave.

"We got through it, alright. Glad it's over and we can get back to some sort of normality," says Paul.

Dave doesn't reply, but reaches out his right arm, and pats Paul on the back as Paul changes from first into second, into third and finally into top as they head off towards the north of the peninsula. The two men in the back lean forward and pat him too.

At the wheel, Paul understands this gesture that his co-volunteers have developed. It's easier than speaking. Sometimes there are no words. He doesn't know if it's a man thing. His wife tells him it is. Either that, or every man she's ever come across is probably on the spectrum.

He keeps telling her that this is politically incorrect but is perhaps true. And anyway, he doesn't want to talk. It can't bring him back. The only person he can talk to about it is his wife and she says that it is all sucking her dry, and she has to keep their little boy going. This is his family now.

Just after first light, on a late December morning, driving to an estuary beach in south Wales, he feels a long way from his old life in New Zealand. It used to be solely the air miles on a map that separated him from his estranged son, and that he was never more than a twenty-four-hour plane journey away. Now the absence that used to be explained – and excused – by physical distance makes the reality of what's actually happened impossible to comprehend.

As he drives towards the beach, the four of them remain sealed in silence in the Coastguard jeep. Yet it's not a difficult silence. More the easy silence of men who are a team and have a task to do that they've been well-trained and drilled to execute. When the shout comes and the pager goes off, they put on their blue dungarees, step into their boots and their yellow, high-vis jackets and respond. This time it's possible ordnance spotted the previous day by a couple of walkers. But it was already too late for the team to attend then. The light was failing.

"Holding up alright now, Paul?" says Dave, glancing towards Paul's foot on the pedal and sniffing.

"Me or the vehicle, mate?" asks Paul. "Seriously, it's a 61 reg. It's criminal the crap we have to put up with in these conditions."

And all the men nod their heads in agreement.

"It's seen us through the last ten years alright," says Dave. "Just pray it sees us through today."

"My days of praying are done with," says Paul, as he indicates to turn off the main road to pick up the rough track through the broadleaf trees to the beach.

Even though it is officially daylight, a thick gloom engulfs Paul and the men as they emerge from the woodland. The weather seems to have been like this for days, perhaps weeks. Not cold, but and mild and murky, with no trace of colour other than the grey that's fudging his vision, making the horizon between sea and sky indistinguishable. With the tide full out, and no movement in the air, there's an empty stillness that's hollower than usual on this Godforsaken shore.

"What's the GPS on this situation?" asks Paul as he navigates the sand just below the high water mark.

"Not far now. Co-ordinates indicate it to be located just by the spit."

Paul ensures the vehicle is in first for this final leg, the clutch is still slipping, engaging and disengaging the engine. He just hopes it will hold up long enough, as he peers into the distance, his hands tight on the steering wheel.

The headlights are still on full beam, picking out the ribs of half-hidden shipwrecks poking through the sand, the odd dead gull, the bleached bones of a strange, long-dead finned creature that he can't name which must have found itself stranded here and whose eyes have long been pecked from its sockets. In the far distance, is the rusty, criss-cross iron latticing of the derelict lighthouse, and up close, within touching distance almost, are the two metal posts of the stark sign with the black warning triangle and the images of projectile objects: a poor graphic attempt at an explosion, of utter chaos, designed to warn people that on this stretch of sand there is likely danger remaining from WW2. Just because things are buried, they're not gone.

Paul brings the vehicle to a stop and the men get out and slog through the sand to the co-ordinates of the reported item. He finds a peculiar comfort in the odd language the team and him use to communicate when they actually do talk. Functional language. Devoid of emotion. Yet it bands them together. For item, see shell or bomb. For ERW that has been reported, see Explosive Remnants of War. It's not dissimilar to the jargon of the police when they rang him from New Zealand in the middle of the night. For fatality, see death by dangerous driving.

The four men stand at the item that they have succeeded in locating, only it isn't just the one shell, but three which must have come to the surface when the strong offshore that blew through a few weeks ago scoured the sand that had disguised their presence beneath.

Paul looks at the items as Dave takes photos with his mobile. The shells are smaller than he'd imagined. He feels let down in a way. He'd expected – and hoped – to find something that might shake his very being when exploded, for the sound of the blast to destroy the unearthly silence here and jolt him into some other state of mind. Instead, the big guys at the EOD Milford (for EOD see Explosive Ordnance Disposal) would have to come (for come, see attend) to detonate two of these pathetic excuses for shells and to take (for take, see transport) the third – possibly chemical – back to their base for destruction.

He thinks of his base (for base, see home) and his wife and how her talking helps him heal. But she's tired with it all. With all the jargon and the acronyms. (For EOD, see End of Discussion).

It doesn't really get light all day as the team waits for the official EOD. They can't leave unattended items however small. They each deal with the drag of time in their own distinctive way. Paul walks. And keeps on walking. The physical movement helps to a certain degree. He has to focus on putting one foot in front of another to keep on going and breathing deeply to release the pain in his diaphragm. Trapped love, his wife calls it. Love with nowhere to go. (For trapped love, see grief).

Everything is upside down and back to front on this Welsh beach in a different hemisphere and at a different latitude. It's winter here at 51 degrees north: summer there at 37 degrees south. There the light is bright. Unforgiving. When he first came here, his new wife told him that the water went down the bath plughole in a clockwise direction unlike anticlockwise in New Zealand. He didn't know whether to believe her. She also told him to tell the son he'd left back home, that if they each took a spade and dug down as deep as they could into the sand when they went to the beach, they'd eventually reach each other. But they never did. They didn't even pick up their spades.

From the edge of the tide that is coming in, Paul can see that the EOD team has now arrived and is with his own team at the side of the Mitsubishi. He picks his way across the mud flats, taking care to avoid the concentric circles of bubbling quicksand. He's heard that people have been sucked away out here without trace. The local cockle pickers say that's why the cockles sing.

His feet take him towards firmer sand, and he crunches

through the shingle and the desiccated seaweed draped around old tree trunks. The sound of the men's voices in discussion and the smell of coffee from a flask is carried in the dank air, and pulls him forward.

Paul stands back as the EOD carries out what they term a controlled explosion to dispose of the two shells and make the area as safe as they can for the time being. It is nothing more than a slight pop and puff, less dramatic than the Mitsubishi back-firing. It leaves only a slight charring on the fine sand after the EOD clears the debris. They will take it back to base along with the suspect chemical shell.

Operation complete, the volunteer team climbs back in the 4×4 and Paul reassumes his position at the wheel. He starts her up, and the engine turns over. He makes sure that the clutch is fully depressed as he tries putting it into first gear. He knows already. He can tell by the feel in his leg, the sound of it, the smell of burnt toast, the way the vehicle won't budge.

"Mechanical failure?" asks Dave.

"If you mean is it buggered, yes it is," says Paul.

"It's not your fault," says Dave.

"Isn't it?" asks Paul. "I don't know . . . Anyway, I'll try to sort it out. You wait here."

Later, Paul makes his way back on a tractor, standing legs astride behind the farmer, his hands firmly placed on the farmer's shoulders for support. The light is fading fast and won't hold out much longer, and the tide is edging closer.

"Be alright, boy," the farmer says, as they drive through the gap in the dunes. "We'll have her out of here in no time. Don't you worry. You just get back with your team."

Back inside the jeep the men are quiet. Paul had anticipated some blame and hostility; but they are simply calm and smiling.

"No point getting all worked up about nothing," says Dave. "Not the end of the world."

Paul clears the windscreen with the arm of his jacket and watches the farmer take control, attaching the rope from the winch at the back of the tractor to the towing eye at the front of the jeep with a hitch knot. Paul winds down his window and strains his head to listen out for instructions as to what to do next.

"Just put your hands on the wheel and steer. No need to drive. Leave it to me. I'll pull away slowly and let the tow rope out gently," says the farmer. "Just take it easy."

Paul does as he's told. He feels the car inch its way forward and he knows that the farmer is in complete control. He eases his grip on the wheel and goes with the motion. He'll be home soon. The three men around him slap him on the back, almost at the same time, as if they've been remotely programmed to do it in synchrony by some unknown maker of men's body language. It is a firmer gesture than the morning's pat and Paul is well aware of the meaning. He looks in the rear view mirror and sees a slight rip in the sky, where a feint blue patch is struggling to make it through the grey.

Too Far Up and
Too Far Down

YOU LET HIM take your hand as you pick your way
across the rocks. His feels thinner-fingered, smoother-
skinned, and the grasp less tight than that of the man you've
left at home. This man is leading you across the temporary
causeway between the mainland and the tidal island. It's
dangerous ground here: underfoot the jagged limestone
is pooled with the ebbing tide and bearded with slippery,
green kelp and there's a strong on-shore gusting straight
into your face that's affecting your balance. Perhaps your
judgement. You really shouldn't be here at all, dicing with
the short time allowed between the low and high Atlantic
tide as it funnels up the Bristol Channel. You've heard
people who've dared to take risks have been swallowed
whole.

You already wish you'd dressed for both purpose and
part, in pull-down hat and large sunglasses; but you'd
wanted to feel the force of the south-westerly full-frontal.
You'd tease out the tangles in your hair later. You'd wanted
the sting of the salt wind on your cheeks, the smarting in
your eyes, knowing that you could wipe away the tears

when they would start to fall. But now you feel as starkly exposed as the carboniferous limestone beneath your old-fashioned, brown-leather walking boots which you've taken out of the cupboard where they've lain unused for far too long. Good as new.

Your companion has come incognito: a tight, grey beanie and on-trend Oakley shades obscuring most of his lovely face except for the straggling wiry whiskers on his upper lip and chin. If he pulled the zip of his grey Microlight jacket up any further, you reckon he'd disappear altogether. Perhaps that's the plan. You wonder whether he's deliberately chosen this colour for camouflage so that in an emergency, such as spying someone he didn't want catching sight of him – or you – he could merge into the early autumn landscape that today is smudging the edge between land and sea. He reminds you of an elusive seal pup that you hope you'll catch sight of once you reach the inner head. With the half-grey hair of a woman in transition whose body is encased in a quilted, black Puffa coat, you wonder what you remind him of.

"It's fine," you say as you let go of his hand. "You go at your own pace. I'll take my time and catch you up."

"You sure?" he asks.

"Sure."

But you're not certain of anything anymore and you feel almost semi-detached in this terrain that's not quite anywhere and will disappear as if it never existed in just over five hours' time.

You sit on a barnacled rock and run your palm across its surface simply to feel its roughness. You pick up a razor shell and stir the waters of the pool at your feet, watch the agitation spread from its centre out. You breathe in the tang of the briny air, aiming to fill your lungs to bursting point to keep you going. A child again, one by one, you pop the desiccated, black pods of seaweed that is swathed across your lap like widows' weeds. The action is soothing and compelling, and you lose yourself in the doing of it.

"Beth! Come on! It's great here!" he's shouting from where he's stopped half-way up the steep slope ahead.

Why you had introduced yourself to the members of the art class as Beth back then, you don't know. But it stuck. The man waving to you from the rock face has never known you by any other name. Your husband has always called you Lizzie. Little Lizzie Lloyd. He's not a bad man at all. It's just . . .

You clamber up the rocks, conscious that your breathing is laboured and your face red. These days, the flush seems to cover your whole body, the seen and the as-yet-unseen-by-this-man parts. He reaches out for you to haul you up the final few yards; but you decline the offer.

"I can manage on my own, thanks," you say. Though you wonder if you actually could.

A woman like you, of your age, is not looking for a helping hand, or any kind of sympathy. That's why you're here. For a fleeting feel of something else. Life is what seems to be happening to everyone else around you: your husband's ever-progressing career, your children's marriages, the births of their children. Even your parents seem free-range, constantly gadding about the world on everlasting cruises with the silver-haired over-eighties. Yet, everything for you seems to be un-happening. You feel sandwiched between other generations' dreams, like a layer in the rocks around you, trapped forever in geological time.

As you near your man he strokes the hair out of your eyes, kisses your forehead. It is not unpleasant. Yet not as you had imagined it when you'd agreed to this sortie organised with military precision: two cars, separate arrivals, remote destination. You are on a mission; yet you are unsure of what you want to accomplish.

Your reach the summit of the inner head where it is flat and grassy. As you walk side by side seaward, you try to control your breathing: in, two, three, four; out, two, three, four, in an attempt to bring your heat rate down without him knowing how much you are struggling, how much you are pretending. What are you trying to prove?

"It's fantastic here, Beth. Can't believe I haven't been here before," he says.

"Beautiful," you say, as you stand motionless and watch the guillemots almost within touching distance. You feel as if one of those black birds is trapped inside your sternum, its wingbeat pounding against your ribcage in a frenzy to take flight.

This vantage point gives you a strange perspective on things, present and past melding in front of you. Down below, where the outgoing tide has exposed a vertical, black fissure, you see a young woman with her new husband, leaning back against the rock-face, laughing. They've made love in the magical, cavernous space that the retreating sea had offered them as a gift. And with not a soul in sight, they'd accepted it. You wonder where that woman went; when the exact moment was that things changed.

"Penny for them," he says. "Better get a move on. Haven't got all day."

You walk, trying to adapt to a new rhythm with this semi-stranger. But your feet seem to be out of step, rooted in the peculiar tempo you once shared with your husband.

As you reach the end of the inner head, you say that you don't think you should venture any further. It's more difficult from this point onwards: the grass disappears and instead, pock-covered limestone stretches all the way to the end of the outer head. You don't have the stomach anymore, to crawl on your hands and knees across Devil's Arch that connects inner with outer, and look down into the surging ocean two hundred feet below.

He doesn't insist. You appreciate this. Instead, he suggests you sit and take in the views, have a bite to eat. He's come prepared with sandwiches and will set up a makeshift camp. You laugh as he takes off his backpack like a Boy Scout and pulls out a small drawstring bag from which he conjures a pink tent with bendy poles that is set up in seconds. The sight of it is a symbol of the other life he leads when he's not on this illicit adventure with a woman he hardly knows. You hardly know yourself.

He opens the flaps, ties them back, and with a pat of his hand on the nylon groundsheet, beckons you to sit down inside.

"I feel ridiculous," you say, as you join him on the floor.

"You're not ridiculous," he says. "Relax."

You are trying to for God's sake. He pours you a cup of milky coffee from the Thermos flask he takes out of the backpack. He offers you a sandwich from his Tupperware container. With the wind beginning to get up outside, and the nylon of the tent rippling, you feel momentarily safe and warm, and disconnected from the mainland and all the life that goes on there.

You don't say a word, but he's close now, his arm against your arm, the warmth radiating through the fabric of his jacket and your coat. And you are aware of his scent, a potent mix of unfamiliar aftershave, astringent and citrus, and a feint odour of sweat. You shift away, shuffling on your haunches towards the gaping door, and place your feet firmly on the grass outside, your hands clasped around your bent knees.

"What's the matter, Beth?" he asks.

"Nothing," you say. "I just need some air."

He lets you be. He's not a bad man either. It's just . . .

You look down to the sea, catch sight of your imagined face for a minute, over-large and distorted, mirrored in its surface. It's a version of a woman you don't recognise anymore, a reflection of what you are becoming. You'd never thought of yourself as a bad woman either, until now.

Your thoughts are interrupted not by the sight and sound of a seal pup that you'd dreamed you'd see, but by a solitary sheep that's lost its footing and is stranded on a ledge half way down the cliff. It's stamped with a red brand and a length of spiteful bramble trails from its fleece. Its bleat is pitiful. You wonder how it ended up in this position. Logic tells you it's too far down to be rescued from above, too far up to be saved from below. And anyway, the cost would be too high to even think of calling out the Coastguard Services and putting their Team at risk for the sake of a worthless old ewe. You know that the creature will remain there in no-man's land until it doesn't stand there anymore. Until its will to live peters out.

"There's nothing you can do about it," says the man. "Look away. Pretend you haven't seen it."

"I can't," you say. "I just can't."

"It's not just the ewe, is it, Beth?" he asks.

"No, it's not just the ewe," you reply, turning to look at the sheep once more.

"Let's make a move. Go home. It doesn't matter. You just don't belong here; with me."

You stand looking out to the horizon. A front is moving in fast and the wind is gusting more strongly now. The tide will soon be on the turn. You wish you'd brought that hat. Wish you'd worn those sunglasses. You turn your back to the wind and feel it pushing into the small of your back, wondering what it might be like if it suddenly knocked you off your feet, gathered you up and whisked you away to who knows where.

You watch the man deal with the temporary love nest. Bendy pole by bendy pole, he dismantles the play tent and folds up the deflated fabric, pressing all the air out of it, putting everything back in his rucksack, in its proper place.

Even though the wind is propelling you forward, the walk seems longer on your return to the mainland. There's an uncomfortable silence between you that you feel you need to fill, but he tells you that it's alright, you don't have to say anything.

Back on the beach he says goodbye and tells you to take care, and ruffles your hair affectionately as you would a puppy. As you are about to move away, a gust of wind blasts sand across your face. You feel the grit between your teeth.

You finger your temples and touch the grains where they're adhering to your hairline.

But it's the left eye that causes the problem. You suddenly remember why you'd always chastise your children for throwing sand on those family days out right where you're standing now. You place your upper eyelashes between your thumb and index finger and tug in an attempt to position the higher lid over the lower one – apparently this trick is designed to soothe and expel any foreign object. But it doesn't seem to be solving the problem.

"Can I help?" he asks.

"No. There's nothing you can do," you say. "It'll be alright. I'll sort it out properly when I get home."

The wind slams the driver's door shut and seals you inside your familiar, little hatchback. You press lock. At the wheel you pull down the visor, slide open the vanity mirror. The offending eye is pricking, and already showing the tell-tale redness of irritation. You try not to rub and aggravate it; but it's impossible. You turn on the ignition and head for home.

You know your husband will be waiting for your return; table set, wine in the fridge, supper at the ready. He'll be eager to hear about the day's events with your art class. And you'll fabricate what happened, stitch by stitch. He'll notice your eye and that expression of honest concern will darken his face. He'll take a dining chair and place it with its back to the kitchen sink and you'll sit there while he drapes a towel around your shoulders, tucking it firmly under your chin. *Lean your head back*, he'll say; and you'll do as you're asked. Then he'll take the egg-cup and fill it with salty, tepid water and he'll say, *try not to blink*. And you'll stare, wide-eyed at the ceiling as he gently bathes your troubled eye. *There. All done,* he'll say. *Leave it settle down. You're lucky, you know. It could have been a lot worse.*

Roasting Leather

I'LL BE SIXTY-SIX exactly when I pull down my scarlet-silk knickers and moon at the throngs of lunch-time shoppers wedged into the pedestrianised precinct. I'll have just stepped out of the main branch of HSBC Bank, Swansea where I'll have collected my State Pension for the first time even though I'm perfectly capable of having it paid into my online account. It will be the 6th September 2023 and I'll be seeking maximum exposure. So I let them have it, full on; my bare arse.

Until that moment, I'll have been a dutiful and law-abiding citizen, the type of person who would quake at the flash of a blue light. But when that official letter comes informing me about changes to the State Pension Age, and I read that *they've* suddenly decided, without adequate warning, to make me wait even longer for my pittance, I see red.

And out of the red mist emerges a scary vision of my future. The job would be first. *Natural wastage* they'd call it age: discrimination legislation, just empty words in a sea of corporate jargon. Redundancy would come uninvited, rat-a-tat-tatting on my door, the way that I'd have to continue knocking on doors, touting employability like a hooker, writing scores of grovelling job applications and pleas for apprenticeships that would be responded to with, *Sorry, we regret to inform you that . . .*

Next would be my home that I'd have worked to buy and run alone since the divorce. Unpaid bills will be spilling over the edges of my pending tray, cracks will open in the render, the monotonous drip of the kitchen tap; a gale-blown roof slate lying in shards on my once manicured lawn, now choking with thistle. Powerless, I'd stand by and watch, a mere spectator.

No doubt then *they* will advise me to seek alternative accommodation. I'd see the *For Sale* sign, prospective punters traipsing over my threshold. The deal done, ownership would be stripped bare. Pound by pound, a life-time's savings frittered away. *They'd* tell me I'd be allowed to keep just £50k; though they'd take away most of my pension too. Pocket-money would be meted out. A child once more.

My imaginings become too much. I feel a tightness in my chest. Crippled by fear and craving security, I decide to dictate the course of my own future.

At first I consider taking Holy Orders. After all, I enjoy the company of women. I'd get somewhere to live, free of charge. There would be the luxury of time for thought, reading and study, perhaps art. But I'm not drawn to the habit and the wimple, or the fact that there would be no contact with the opposite sex.

Next, life on the road perhaps. Abandon all my worldly goods and hobo my way through life, on the hoof, an eternal pilgrim. I've seen Sadhus swathed in tangerine, barefooted, and intent on their journeying. But the barefoot doesn't appeal.

I grudgingly work out that I won't be able to afford the everlasting cruising I've seen in the *Saga* adverts – smug, silver-haired couples with toothy smiles, on deck with the sun in their face. I'm not partial to nightly fine-dining either, or to being seated top-table, having to schmooze with the Captain; so I discard this option.

I finally crack it. I'd be able to vent my pent up angst at the world, make a political point and at the same time carve myself a new future. *They'd* have to act in the end. I'd keep on until I forced their hand.

So that day hence, outside the bank, people will laugh when they see a sixty-something woman, with her red knickers around her ankles. *Poor old biddy,* they'll say. The patrol cars will come then, the *Heddlu*. armed with a blanket which they'll wrap around me for my own good so I don't offend public taste. *Come on, Love,* they'll say, *let's get you home.* But they won't press charges this first time.

I'll make a habit of gross indecency so they'll start to threaten me with warnings, court appearances and talk of fines. But I won't want rebukes. I'll want revenge.

I'm not like *her* who sucks off her spouse, never done a day's work in her life. *She* who's stolen the twenty-eight-year pension I earned for doing time with *him*. The law was different then; but I've never said a word. Now deeds will surpass words.

It'll be towards the end of October, 2023 when I drive to the seaside village on the south side of Gower, where they live like puffed-up peacocks. The evenings will have drawn in by then and I'll tip-toe along the gravel drive towards the house that uses so much lighting that it must visible from Pluto. Her car will be parked outside. I've often seen her drive the silver, gas-guzzling Toyota with its over-sized tyres and its swanky, chrome bull-bars. The familiar registration will be in front of me: KAR 1.

At first, I'll take the fifty-pence piece from my pocket. I like the shape. I'll make a start on the driver's door and scratch my way around; a perfect circumference. I'll love the sound of metal on metal and under the stars, I'll finger the deep grooves that I've etched. Minute by minute, I'll become bolder, the rush of adrenaline surging through my tired body. There'll be more pleasure going on here in a few minutes than I'll have had in decades. Deeper and deeper, I'll carve; gouging *Karly is a cunt* into the metallic paint. Under my breath, I'll mouth it over and over again. Won't want to alert them, just yet. A few minutes more, just to wallow in the thrill of it all.

The petrol will be in a rusty-red jerry can that I'll have filled to capacity from South Road Services. I'll hear the expensive fuel slosh around as I'll pick it up and pour it lovingly, drop by precious drop, over the sleek, silver body-work. Using the nozzle, I gently drip it through the open window that they've conveniently left open for me. The petrol will form pools on the cream, leather seats where she has placed that young, fat arse of hers. I've always liked the distinctive smell of freshly stuck matches, so I'll keep striking the heads of the extra-long *Swan* matches against the hard emery board surface of the box. I'll listen to the friction, wonder at the chemical reaction; the combination of red phosphorous and black carbon. I'll watch them ignite and sniff the evening air, the waft of burning Sulphur in my nostrils.

It won't take long before KAR 1 is ablaze, completely

licked with flame. I'll stand back and observe the inferno. I'll see the metal twist; lose its sheen and its spangling gleam. I'll inhale the stench of petrol and roasting leather. And I'll feel all the tension that's been welling-up in me for far too long, seep from my body.

The police will be called to the scene of the crime soon after KAR 1 and COL 1 see me, not lurking in shadow, but lit up by the conflagration. I won't offer any resistance as they cuff me and escort me to the back of the squad car. The blue light will be flashing; and this time it will be for me. That night I'll spend my first night safe behind bars.

Of course, there'll be a trial and naturally, I'll be found guilty and to be of sane mind. By 2023, women will be able to be incarcerated at Swansea Jail, which I'd been hoping for for such a long time. It never made sense to me that women had to go to prison outside Wales, so far from home. I'd always thought what a wonderful position Swansea Prison enjoyed there on the front: uninterrupted views out over Swansea Bay, the hills of north Devon beyond.

I'll be content in my new abode. I'll have my own cell with all mod-cons and en-suite. It will be squeaky clean, so much nicer somehow than all those horrible *Care Homes* I feared I'd live in one day, that greeted you with the tang of urine and moist carpets. I won't be one of those name-less, faceless people that *Wales Today* insists on showing on the half-past-six news when they talk about the over-50s: lazy journalists with their stereotypical images focusing on wrinkled liver-spotted hands, rolled-down tights and slippers, a Zimmer frame, a piggy-bank on a mantelshelf, or a clasp-purse spilling a few pathetic coins onto a table-top. The food won't be great, but as my mother once used to say of hotels: *it's nice to have it put in front of you*. If I get ill, I'll have the comfort of knowing that a doctor will see me immediately. No more NHS waiting lists. No more financial worries. No more invisible me.

Plenty of Time, Jane

Mrs. Tucker was flat on her back in the driveway. She was there because her husband had run her over. She had her left arm stretched out and was clinging onto the ivy that she noticed was rampant and quite out of control along the dry stone wall. She was thinking that if it had been husband number one who had done this, she might have understood. That it was her second husband came as quite a shock to Mrs. Tucker. But, there you go.

She guessed he didn't even know how it happened. Mrs. Tucker could see the local policeman, Jim, who did 'cuppa with a copper' in the village hall once a month, asking Mr. Tucker to give his version of events and breathalysing him in the lane. Mrs. Tucker wanted to tell Jim that Mr. Tucker must have been completely oblivious of what had happened from his perspective: inside the 4×4, the radio blaring, the sensors bleeping: He wouldn't have seen, or heard, anything until it was too late. Mrs. Tucker was also thinking what a complete waste of money it had been to go for the sensors on the 4×4, back and front. But she didn't say a word.

As she lay on the slate chippings. Mrs. Tucker thought back to what a lovely day it had been earlier. She didn't want to think of the night before, when he'd called her a miserable old cow over supper and kept on about her really having to have that one more glass of wine. Not a breath of air that morning, blue sky, blazing sun: perfect. No sign of a change either. She'd had all the windows in the studio open and had gone out on the balcony to breathe in the view.

Mr. Tucker had been at his desk, head down, working hard as Mrs. Tucker had said: *I've never seen Gower from the air. Have to do it one day.* Mr. Tucker didn't say anything in response. Mrs. Tucker thought how strange that she'd wished that and now the air ambulance was on its way to her. Her mother's pronouncements came into her head: *Be careful what you wish for, young lady.* She couldn't work out how long ago that had been. Time seemed to be ticking to a different beat there on the drive. She tried to maintain focus. August 28th 2014. It was then that Mrs. Tucker realised that this date would be forever etched in Mr. Tucker's memory whatever happened in the end. He never used to be any good with dates.

Mrs. Tucker put it down to Mr. Tucker rushing. Even though he got up early every morning, whenever they had to be somewhere by a certain time, she'd always have to chivvy him. *Get your shoes on, Tom. We're going to be late*, she'd say. *Plenty of time, Jane*, he'd say, *plenty of time.* She sometimes wondered whether he did it on purpose, just to annoy her. And now look. It had come to this. Her in pieces in their very own garden.

Mrs. Tucker had decided not to go to the 4 o'clock meeting. It was a few miles away at the pub – The Dolphin – just off the village green at Llanrhidian. She'd made up her mind straight after he'd gone on and on at her over supper. He could do it on his own for a change. They'd worked with Carol, the owner, before so it wasn't as if it was difficult. She'd stay at home, finish up in the studio, and then do the prep as she usually did for the new fish dish Mr. Tucker had taken to cooking: cod with borlotti beans and chorizo. Mr. Tucker used to refer to Mrs. Tucker in company as his little sous chef. In private, Mrs. Tucker called it skivvying. She was going to de-seed and slice a red chilli, peel and grate stem ginger, crush garlic and slice the spring onions. Then, when Mr. Tucker got home, he would simply have to put it all together et voila! She'd been looking forward to that.

There in her garden, Mrs. Tucker squinted in the sunlight at the five-bar farm gate, held on the iron hook now. She screamed, *Bloody gate. Why the fuck didn't you ever get around to doing it properly?* Mr. Tucker was still being interviewed by Jim, and they both looked around when she said this. Mrs. Tucker noticed that Mr. Tucker's face was blanched and was sparkling with beads of sweat. The paramedic told her to try and keep calm as he inserted a catheter into her right hand and got her started on the morphine.

Mrs. Tucker wondered why she'd even offered to hold the gate instead of using the hook. Then she remembered it had been twenty to four and Mr. Tucker had been flapping around, getting his folder together, scrabbling for the car keys, accusing her of putting them somewhere safe – too safe – searching for his asthma pump and saying, *Is that the time already?* So, Mrs. Tucker had stood like a mute sentry at the gate opening it in readiness for him to come down the steep drive, and out into the single-file lane with the sheep and the odd passing tractor. Her doing this would save Mr. Tucker having to get out and shut it after him. And he'd get to the meeting on time.

Mr. Tucker didn't know he'd taken Mrs. Tucker's knees with him as he passed her, holding back the gate. Mrs. Tucker didn't realise either until she'd looked down and seen her shabby grey leggings flapping along with the skin and the blood pouring down the fabric. She hated those leggings and they didn't match her top either. Mr. Tucker had always told her she'd looked vile in them and that she didn't dress for him anymore whatever that meant. They were not the sort of clothes she should have been wearing for an accident.

At that point, Mrs. Tucker wasn't feeling any pain and was still on her feet. Her intention had been to let Mr. Tucker know what had happened before he drove off. That's why Mrs. Tucker had decided to slam the palm of her right hand on the tail-gate of the 4×4 to get him to stop. It was obvious that Mrs. Tucker needed medical help at that point – some analgesic, antiseptic – twenty or so stitches at the very most. Patching up. But nothing more.

Mrs. Tucker had been thinking that at last she'd have to throw the offending article of clothing away. She had also been thinking she'd have to get Carol on Mr. Tucker's mobile and let her know that Mr. Tucker wouldn't be able to make the meeting for 4 o'clock as he'd promised as there'd been a bit of a blip and that Mr. Tucker had to take her in the car to A & E. Mrs. Tucker also realised that she'd have to think about something else for supper. Perhaps a take-away on the way home from A & E as current statistics indicated that they'd likely be there for over four hours. A take-away would have been a welcome treat for Mr. and Mrs. Tucker, living where they did in the sticks. Even at that point, with the gaping knee-wounds, Mrs. Tucker was quite looking forward to that and would have gone for the usual: chicken kahari done in the skillet and pilau rice and Naans. She would have put the cod in the fridge. They could have had that the next day, rather than waste it.

Mr. Tucker could not have heard Mrs. Tucker's palm on the back of the 4×4 and he hadn't seen her there behind, as he reversed to straighten the car out as he knew he'd obviously taken it to close to the wall. He'd heard a sound which he presumed was steel on stone not steel on bone. Mrs. Tucker had always gone on about not relying on the sensors, but instead, turning and looking over the shoulder to reverse. *Wasn't that the way we taught back in the old days?* she used to say.

So, Mr. Tucker reversed into Mrs. Tucker (at relatively low speed), hitting her in the pelvic region and felling her before the rear-offside tyre ploughed its deep-rubbered tread across Mrs. Tucker's temples. Under the car, Mrs. Tucker thought she was a goner straight away. As she saw the tyre's black surface in stark close-up, smelled the horse dung all over it and felt the grey slate chippings from the drive that had embedded themselves in the grooves, she remembered thinking, *There's going to be no coming back from this. I'm fucking dead.*

Mrs. Tucker could hear Jim the policeman saying that the 'victim' (she, Mrs. Tucker) must have self-extricated from under the vehicle and rolled to the position where she was on the drive. Mrs. Tucker thought how strange was the language the emergency services used. She'd never heard the term, *self-extricated*. But it was true. She had somehow managed to slide herself out from under the car before Mr. Tucker got out. She could only manage a few yards as there was piercing pain in her pelvis so the paramedics were putting her in a pelvic binder as a precaution. Mrs. Tucker had never felt such tightness in her life. They said it was *precautionary* in case there was any internal bleeding.

Mrs. Tucker was also aware of Jim the policeman asking Mr. Tucker why he'd moved the car from the scene of the accident. Mr. Tucker explained that just after it happened, The Tesco delivery van approached from one direction and the builders' van from the other and they were beeping their horns and getting impatient and he'd felt an asthma attack coming on. So Mr. Tucker had moved the car into a tiny triangle of land outside the garden gate so that the traffic in the single lane could get through, he said. Mrs. Tucker knew this to be the case. She remembered the logo on the side of the Tesco van: *you shop, we drop* and found it quite ironic that this was the first response of sorts. She also remembered the young driver's face. He took one look at the sixty-something woman lying in the drive and went about his work. It was gone four by then. It irritated Mrs. Tucker that Jim kept on referring to the 4×4 as an Audi Q5 when in fact it was an Audi Q7.

Mrs. Tucker wished she'd been unconscious as she started to stress and shout: *Please somebody make all this unhappen.* She'd never used that word in her life before – it was though she was pleading for an old Betamax video to be rewound. To go back to the beginning. To start again. She was convinced she was dying and kept asking the paramedic if she was. *Not on my watch*, he kept saying, *not on my watch*, as they wedged her into the gurney and the head and body immobilising boards. She'd never vomited from a horizontal position before and they had to release the tape across her face and tip her sideways so she could wretch onto the drive. She was in a terrible state about that, worrying who would clear it up, and the surgical gloves and syringes which were now littering her lovely garden. She insisted that everything be taken away before her daughter got there as she'd have a fit about the mess with her OCD. She had a latex allergy and operating theatres had to be latex-free on the three occasions she'd had C-sections. Mrs. Tucker suddenly saw her three granddaughters' faces smiling at her. Was it only a few days ago when they'd hosed each other down as well as the Audi in the glorious summer sunshine until they were wet through?

Won't be long now, the paramedics kept telling Mrs. Tucker as they were waiting for the air ambulance. It was going to come down in the field at the bottom of the garden. Mrs. Tucker felt cheated that she wasn't well enough for this first air trip over Gower. They were taking her to the University Hospital of Wales in Cardiff. It was in her best interest, they said. She thought how impressed her mother would be with the scale of her injuries and how she'd been taken to a trauma unit in the capital city. *Dw i'n mynd i'r prifddinas. Dw i'n mynd i'r prifddinas.** Mrs Tucker kept repeating and laughing out loud, wondering whether she was using the correct mutation after *yr*, but not really caring anymore.

---

* I'm going to the capital

Though Mrs. Tucker started to fixate on small things: the nail of her right little finger which had been broken in the accident. *Get me my emery board, Tom*, she shouted. *Quick. You've ruined my fucking nails*. She didn't think it was at all strange that she was focusing on something so small when everything else was obviously in bits. Mrs. Tucker was also worrying that:

A She'd pegged a load of washing out and who would bring it in;

B the bins wouldn't be taken out the next day;

C the figs that were heavy and bruised on the tree, would remain there unpicked; and,

D no one would pack a bag for the hospital.

Mr. Tucker said that he'd do all these things and that Mrs. Tucker could cross them off her worry list. He'd come to the hospital in the car later with the rest of the family. He kept saying to Mrs. Tucker: *Stay with me, darling. Please stay with me, darling*. Mrs. Tucker had never heard him speak like this before and she felt really sorry for him as he took her hand and kneeled down beside her. She noticed that a crowd of village people had gathered in the lane by then and were standing there with their arms folded, enjoying the scene, waiting for the helicopter to arrive.

Mrs. Tucker could never have imagined that there was such beauty in impending death and that life could be so beautiful; so intense. There were gulls above her and she realised that despite living in her home by the sea for all those years, she'd never really taken notice of them before, not *really* taken notice of them: the way they soared above her on the thermals, their strange squeal splitting the silence of the afternoon.

But it was the warmth Mrs. Tucker relished. She could feel the sun's rays penetrating her damaged face. And there was a strange off-shore breeze that had suddenly got up: it carried a sweet honeysuckle scent off the land. And then all Mrs. Tucker wanted to do was lower her lids and drift off to sleep.

With the world shuttered out, the last thing Mrs. Tucker remembered was the whirr of the approaching helicopter followed by a deafening roar as it came in to land. She felt the air from its blades on her face. And then that ride in the sky just a little too late and not being able to share it with Mr. Tucker, but leaving him there watching as she took flight.

Soft Boiled Eggs

Gordon Pritchard sits down to his boiled egg.

"Most important meal of the day, this," he says, as he does every morning to his wife, Megan, sitting opposite him at the kitchen table. "Can't get by on an empty stomach."

In perfect synchrony, they saw across their respective shells, Megan hoping that she's got his egg just right.

"Not too runny for you, is it?" she asks.

"Did you bring them to a rolling boil?" he asks.

"Course I did," she says. "Just as I always do."

He dips his toast into the yolk, as the white albumen – clear in parts – oozes over the cracked rim, running down the egg-cup onto the plate.

"Look, have mine," she insists.

"No. It's okay. Too late now."

He's attempting to mop up the glair with the bread, before giving up and shoving the plate away from him towards the centre of the table.

"Got much on today?" she asks.

"Drenching first thing and then the AI man's coming," he replies, as he rises from the table, scraping the chair across the flagstones. "See you later for a bit of lunch."

And then he's through the kitchen and into the utility room. Megan hears him sigh as he takes down his green, waterproof dungarees from the pegs and climbs into them, adjusting the braces. His work boots will be next, uppers caked with mud, laces loose and yawning, just waiting to be stepped into.

She listens as the door closes and then gets up to clear the table and carry the dishes to the sink, scraping the eggshells from the plates into the food bin. Through the window, she watches him walk to the sheds, his feet dragging as though they don't want to take him there anymore. He's getting too old for all this, she thinks. as she sets about the washing up. Young man's game.

But there are no young men on the farm. They'd known there never would be. They'd talked about it before the wedding. Marrying a farmer was about business as well as love, a lot of people had told her at the time. *Are you sure?* she'd asked him. *Absolutely,* he'd replied

Through her yellow Marigolds, Megan feels the water in the sink going cold. She wonders if he's ever been able to imagine what life would be like with the passing of the years. What it would be like putting on the worn shoes of an older version of himself, just the two of them yoked together, ticking along on the farm. What he feels when he looks at her these days. She's forgotten how it felt to be young, and so much in love that they never spared a thought for the future. She unplugs the sink and watches the water drain away. It leaves a greasy mark on the white porcelain. She'll give it a good scrub later.

❧

In the sheds, Gordon stands in the press of fleeces stamped with the red Pritchard brand. His arms are outstretched and flapping as he rounds up the sheep into the pens, trying to create some order out of the mayhem, and calm the incessant bleating. He needs to stop the worms and the parasites, prevent the rot setting in.

He could do with another pair of hands: his knees are crocked, his right hip hurts, and his shoulders are stooped with the weight of the years. *Who'd be a bloody farmer?* he curses out loud as he wrestles each struggling ewe to the ground, seizing it round the neck in an arm-lock. He wrenches open the mouth wide to avoid the bite, plunging the drench from the syringe deep into the back of the animal's throat.

He's glad when he hears the growl of the diesel as the Artificial Insemination man pulls into the yard. He's looking forward to having an hour or so of company, even if it's to be spent with a man up to the elbows in rubber gloves inserting semen into the reproductive tracts of heifers. Gordon watches him stride towards the old bowl in the yard and dip his rubber boots in the disinfectant. It's such a sanitary business, all this, he thinks, as he watches him pick up his bucket and his brush and his tool box of insemination implements. Such a lot of paraphernalia to get cows in calf. He never fails to be amazed by the statistics of it all. One bull can produce one hundred doses of semen in just one ejaculation.

"How many we got, today, Gordon?" the AI man asks.

"Ten. Bulling early on," says Gordon. "Whole bloody lot of them mounting."

"Let's get going then," the AI man says.

"Aye," says Gordon, "I'll give you a hand for a bit but I've got a lot on so I'll have to leave you to it."

Gordon takes his stick and ushers each Holstein into the forward-facing crush, clamps its head in the metal lock, so that it is in the perfect position for the AI man to begin the impregnation. There's a straw of semen at room temperature, a sterile coverall, lube and a gun. No need to keep a male on the farm at all. He finds it all so matter of fact the way that the cows are separated from the sires by distance and time, yet acknowledges that the brutal mechanics of it all pay off. The taste of his breakfast egg regurgitates in his throat.

No difference between surrogacy and the AI man, really, she used to say after they married. They'd been in their late-thirties then. *Too late,* he'd said. Though now as he stands aching in the farmyard, he knows that that it mightn't have been too late at all. He can see her there in the kitchen, hormones raging through her soft body, hair dark and glossy, eyes shining with the pleading. *I've got the eggs. You've got the sperm. Just a womb we need. A container,* she'd said. *It wouldn't be the same,* he'd replied. *A man, I am, not a bloody sperm donor.*

And they'd left it at that.

Gordon leaves the AI man to sort the cattle and goes back to the utility room to wash-up before lunch. He always has his on the table at 1 o'clock, just as his father did, just as his father's father had. He can see the long line of Pritchard men sitting there in the kitchen, the ripe, big-bellied women standing on-hand, serving, waiting, round and fecund. Sometimes he's sure he can see all his male ancestors morph into one Pritchard being sitting in his oak carver at the head of the table, the sinewy forearms taunting him, reaching out to pull him in.

And then the chair is empty.

Megan knows by rote the patterns of the day: the boots coming off, the dungarees hung back up, the tap water running into the utility room sink for a full five minutes to free the hands and nails of cloying mud and dirt. All the stuff of the farm. And then him coming into the kitchen and saying: *Something smells nice,* before pulling up his seat, picking up his knife and fork and holding them in his fists, waiting.

She puts his plate in front of him, before settling herself down opposite. She watches as he tucks into his sausage and mash with relish, lowering his head to the fork with every mouthful. He sounds like he is enjoying it; but he doesn't waste time talking. He mops up the onion gravy with great slabs of her homemade bread, wiping the plate clean of very trace.

She leans across the table and pours his tea when he's ready: weak; black; no sugar; the Gower way, he calls it.

"Go alright?" she asks.

"Aye," he says.

"Good," she says.

"He's still there. Nearly done."

"And this afternoon?" she goes on.

"Posts up the top fields need replacing. New stock fencing to go up," he says, getting up in a perfectly choreographed repeat of the morning's actions. "See you for supper."

And then he closes the back door behind him.

She listens to the rev of the quad, and the yap of the collies, before both fade away. The volume seems to have been turned down on her whole life. She's forgotten how it might feel to hear a gentle voice asking what she's got on in the day, what she might like to eat when her chores are done, what she hopes for in the future. She doubts if he ever considers what she might have given up for all this. Perhaps the answers are not those he'd like to hear. Or perhaps this was always part of the unspoken deal she'd bought into as a woman without a womb.

She knows he'd never admit to the void in their lives. Now food seems to fill the vacuum. Though it is only about an hour a day when they actually sit together at the kitchen table to eat it, the rest of the time is spent talking about it or rearing it or growing it or sourcing it or preparing it. She can't put her finger on the time when she started to vex about the saltiness of a slice of ham, whether potatoes were good for mash, or the bread suitable for toasting. And whether his boiled egg was to his taste.

But for now, he's in the top fields, banging in posts where his land adjoins the common. Stock that's been grazing wild, has forced its way through, hoofing up the clover grass and gorging on the edible, wild flowers that he's been re-introducing.

He enjoys it out here, the sense of permanence in the vistas. There's comfort in the swing of the mallet, the monotony of the thud, the sight of the fresh, pale wood he's impaling not yet weathered by time and the elements.

He rests for a moment and leans on the wooden handle and looks down on the farm. It's tucked in tight within the wind-crippled trees which are bent-double by the south-westerlies. It looks as if it's stood there for all of time; as though it's been birthed out of the old red sandstone, of the very earth. He thinks of all the generations that have lived and died within its stone walls, farmed its heavy, damp-brown soils, tended its spiteful blackthorn. He wonders why he struggles to keep on looking after it, who will go on tending it when the time comes.

He sees the yard's empty now, the AI man's Land Rover gone. It's a good job done. By spring his fields will be full of calves and in no more than twenty months, those calves will calve too. It might not be natural, but by God, the whole performance is worth it. His father's words come to mind: *It cannot be, Gordon. With Megan you'll just get old and then you'll die.*

He quickly returns to the task in hand, hammering in the posts along the boundary with an innate rhythm until circles of sweat darken the underarms of his check shirt and bead his leathered brow. He stands back and admires his effort: a perfect line of verticals marking out his land. He bends down and strains to uncoil the new metal stock fence and rolls it out foot by foot. Nail by nail, tap by tap, he attaches it to each post in turn. And when he's done with that, he runs barbed-wire along the top for the whole length. That would keep them out. Ensure his new calves could pasture in his fields. Enable them to grow and thrive and gush forth milk from swollen udders.

The sun is low over the ocean by then, the sky the colour of a placenta. The light won't hold out much longer and it will be impossible for him to go on working. His stomach is groaning, calling him back to the farm. His legs are weary but his feet will walk him back of their own accord. She'll be waiting. Ready to serve up. He's looking forward to the spring lamb they'll be sharing this evening. It's one of theirs.

The Real Thing

THE WOMAN SITS on a pink-leather chair, her feet immersed in the soak-bath set on the raised plinth in front of her. In all of her fifty years, she's never indulged herself like this at three o'clock on a Wednesday afternoon. Even though the water is warm and soothing on her feet, she sits upright in the chair, her shoulders raised around her ears as though she is trying to save herself from drowning.

"You don't look very comfortable there, Mrs Richards," says Samantha, her assigned technician. "Here, let me switch the chair on for you."

"Call me, Liz," says the woman. "Feel like I'm doing something wrong when people call me Mrs Richards or Elizabeth."

"Well, here you go, Liz," says Samantha as she hands her the remote. "You can have it any speed you like. Let rip."

"I'll have a go."

"I'll leave you in the sea-salt there for about quarter-of-an-hour or so, just to soften things up, soothe the aches and pains. Can I get you something to drink while you're soaking?"

"A tea would be nice, please. Weak. No sugar."

"Do you fancy something a bit stronger? Some fizzy?"

"In the afternoon?"

"Yes. In the afternoon. It's not illegal, you know. And it's complimentary."

"Go on then. Just the one."

Samantha returns with a flute of sparkly and places it on the glass-topped table at the side of the chair. She sets the black timer for fifteen minutes.

"I don't want you to get webbed feet," she says as she walks away again towards the kitchen. "I'll be back when the buzzer goes off. I promise!"

While she settles herself in, Liz studies the other women in the salon sitting in identical chairs wondering if she-who-shall-never-be-named might actually be one of them. She's never actually seen her. Just built up an image: thick lustrous hair, immaculate make-up, hands and feet manicured and pedicured on a weekly basis. Young. Full of hormones.

Liz doesn't feel as though she is part of the same species as these women who are fixating on their latest model iPhones and texting non-stop. They are oblivious to their assigned technicians who sit below the plinth, washing and pampering their feet, no words passing between them. She recalls what she was taught as a child in Sunday School about Jesus washing feet. These women, and she-who-shall-never-be-named, have probably never been taught that particular lesson about humility.

Liz raises her glass and says, *Cheers*, to herself, before taking the first sip. The bubbles rise and fizz at the surface, she can feel them tickling her nostrils. It's years since she's had, what the salon calls, champagne, though she knows this is not the real thing. What is anymore? But the effects are just the same, coursing through her veins and up to her brain to produce a beautiful, light-headed rush. The closest thing she's had to this recently is anaesthetic, and the cold flush of an intravenous drip.

She doesn't put the chair on recline as she's afraid that she might drop off; but she opts for the vibration at speed and deep-kneading that the technology promises. The chair works hard on her shoulder blades, along the length of her spine, pummelling each vertebra down to the small of her back and into her coccyx. She feels herself loosening, or maybe unravelling; she can't tell as yet.

Through the long-stemmed glass held close to her face, her feet and ankles look altered: doubly-refracted by alcohol and salt water, they are pale and bloated, just disparate parts, as though she's no longer attached to them. To anything. She wonders if Samantha is right, that with the prolonged immersion of her feet in tepid water, she might adapt and mutate into a creature that could swim instead of walk. A creature that would allow the water to hold its weight.

He always used to tell her she had lovely feet. *Like a thoroughbred racehorse, you are,* he'd say. When her ankles were thin and her toes brown, she'd adorned her left foot with a cheap toe-ring they'd bought from a beach-seller in Bali – a little, pretend silver dolphin that curled around the toe next to her big one.

Later in life, he'd fondle her feet when they watched television – not in a sexual way – but holding them in his lap, caressing them as if by rote, the way their children used to gain comfort from rubbing the satin edges of their special blankets.

Though there were other times, too, in the days and years that went before, when he'd put her young feet in his mouth and suck her toes. She wonders if he's rekindled his love of toe-sucking now that he's shacked up with she-who-shall-never-be-named. Is the whole thirty years she spent with that man – her husband – refracted by memory too, as if there was no truth in any of it at all? For in the end, his feet walked him away from her.

She fixates on the submerged feet. How on earth has she allowed them to get like this? Brittle nails, cracked heels, scaly skin. The hardening callus. She wonders if it is too late. She drains her glass in a quick succession of gulps.

"You're done," says Samantha as she returns to turn off the buzzer, "Nice and relaxed now, are we?"

"Getting there. Bit by bit. But look, I'm sorry about my feet. I've really ley let myself go."

"That's why I'm here. We'll have you sorted in no time."

Liz watches as Samantha sits down on the foot-stool and spreads the towel on her lap. Samantha raises Liz's feet from the water and rests them on the waiting towel. She discards the foot-bath with the water now grown cold, places it out of sight, below the plinth. The woman closes her eyes for a moment as Samantha cradles her feet in the towel, pats them dry, wipes the water from between her toes.

"What d'you think?" Liz asks, looking at her feet in Samantha's hands.

"I've seen worse," says Samantha.

"Rather you than me. I'd have to wear surgical gloves."

"It detracts from the experience. Yours and mine."

"Know what you mean. But d'you think you can save them?"

"The only time it's too late is when you're dead," she laughs. "A little TLC should do it."

Liz feels her shoulders unknot as Samantha holds both her feet. The girl's hands are soft, reassuringly firm, fingers pressing down on the bridges, thumbs pushing up on the arches. Liz watches her, this young stranger at her feet, in this the most intimate of situations. Jesus reincarnate as nail technician, determined to save her soul as well as her feet. After all, she's already turned the expectation of weak tea into fizzy wine – perhaps she can make the debilitated walk too, all-inclusive in the £30 mid-week pedicure.

"Please don't feel you have to talk, you know," says Samantha. "Just allow yourself to be pampered. You deserve it. And you're paying for it."

"Are you sure? I'd just like to watch you, if you're happy with that. It's all new to me."

So Liz absorbs everything: the feel of the file on her soles and heels; the exfoliating scrub on her dried skin. She watches as the debris – little bits of her, the dead and desiccated hardness that has built up over time – float down to be gathered up in the paper tissue Samantha has at the ready. With the dermis gone, a deep layer of pink and pulpy, young flesh makes itself seen underneath, and with it, a new sensation of cream being rubbed deep into her toes, her soles, her ankles, up to her calves in slow, circular movements. She's glad she's not talking; the communication is more intense in the silence. Just the laying on of hands on feet.

She watches as Samantha goes on to massage the

puffiness in her ankles, probing the dimples with the tips of her fingers until the fluid disappears. Her feet feel warmer now as the blood starts to flow and the colour returns. Samantha is right; she deserves this.

But it's the smell. Honey. Coconut oil. She could almost be back on the beach in Bali again, the sun roasting her oiled skin, that little dolphin ring glinting on her toe.

"Not too much for you, is it?" Samantha asks. "Some people find it a bit intense."

"No. I'm fine."

"Good. Right. Time for nails now. Any preference for colour?"

"Leave it to you."

"Coral pink, I think. Set your skin tone off a treat."

Samantha threads the length of cotton wool in and out between Liz's toes. She clips the nails carefully and rounds them off with an emery board, pushes back the cuticles, to reveal half-moons.

"Haven't seen those for a while," says Liz.

"Beautiful. They were there all the time. All they needed was a little seeing-to. You need to watch these nails though, especially this one on the big toe. I don't want you to end up with it in-growing. It can do a lot of damage, cause a lot of pain, something in-growing like that."

"Yes. I know," say Liz, well-aware of the anger that can poison your insides. Unspoken of. Tan-y-a is her name. She-who-shall-be-spoken-of. She rolls the three syllables around her head in an exaggerated fashion. Hardly worth the breath. But there. She's saying it silently. It's a start.

Liz watches as her new nails gradually present themselves to her: polished coral against skin, hydrated and glowing. She's done what she said she would, this girl, Samantha. Salvaged them.

"Transformed," says Samantha. "Just rub in a drop of cuticle oil and you're good to go. Pleased?"

"Yes. I am. You've worked miracles. I felt you would."

"Make sure you don't leave it as long next time."

"No. I won't."

The woman rises from the chair, rolls her trousers back down, steps into her jewelled flip-flops. She takes a moment to look down at her feet. Renewed and crying out for a toe ring. An expensive one this time. Real silver.

"See. I told you. You've got lovely feet," says Samantha as Liz turns to go. "Take you anywhere, those feet, you know."

Gingerbread Men

I F IT WASN'T for the fact that the grandchildren were
flying like snowbirds down south for Christmas, she
wouldn't have been making gingerbread men. Outside,
it was in the upper eighties, but the Floridian heat didn't
bother her even as she stood in her kitchen, sifting flour,
ginger and cinnamon, tapping the sieve rhythmically,
absorbed by the fine dust falling into the mixing bowl.
She added the butter, rubbed the mixture between the
tips of her fingers, lifting it above the rim, watching the
crumbs getting smaller and changing colour. She knew
instinctively when the rubbing needed to stop.

It was when she was kneading the mixture and rolling
it out on the marble countertop that she reached in the
drawer with her floured hands for the gingerbread cutter.
She could have sworn it had been there recently. But time
had ticked to a different beat since he'd been gone. She'd
left the house as she was: grey-blonde hair scraped back
off her face into a scrunchie, no make-up and soon found
herself in the household department at Macy's.

᧞

If it wasn't for the fact that his daughter and her husband and the new baby were flying north from Lauderdale to spend a few days with him at the oceanside condo at Hutchinson Island, he wouldn't have needed the crib and fresh linen. He wanted to show that he meant business this time; that a granddaughter wasn't just for Christmas.

At Macy's he arranged for the high chair to be delivered along with the jungle gym complete with little mirrors and tinkling bells: all the paraphernalia of newborns that he chose to miss out on with his own daughter. But he decided he'd take the Christmas tree with him. Even though it was fake, he couldn't resist it. The package was almost as big as him and he tucked it under his arm and stepped onto the descending escalator.

❧

"Little Greg Benally!" she hollered, pointing her finger at him as he glided past.

He looked back over his shoulder at the sound of her voice coming from the ascending escalator.

"Melissa Griffin!" he shouted. "Hang on there. I'll come back up."

He kissed her gently on the cheek. He remembered her smell.

"I'd know those eyes anywhere," he said. "You haven't changed one bit."

"You're still so full of shit, honey," she said.

Her blue eyes were as soulful as he remembered them thirty-five years earlier when she'd come into the beachside bar at the Holiday Inn. He'd be there Friday evenings jamming big time then: reggae mostly, playing bass left-handed on his Gibson. She'd been long and lean then. Long, lean Melissa. She'd stacked on the pounds since; but yes, the eyes were just the same.

She looked him up and down: the same brittle frame, no fat, lithe like a pre-adolescent. She felt she could crush his bones with a nut cracker. His hair cascaded in dark waves to his shoulders, though as she towered above him, she could see a white streak along the parting. He reminded her of a skunk.

"You're still so God damned skinny, honey" she said. "What you doing that keeps you so thin?"

"Genes," he said.

She guessed it wasn't just the genes. More like the booze, and perhaps still the weed and the caffeine.

"Coffee?" he asked.

"Sure," she said. "Be good to catch up. I'll just grab a gingerbread cutter. See you across the lot. Blueberry muffins to die for."

❧

She was right about the coffee. He took his strong and black. She was intrigued with the sugar as she counted ten little paper tubes that he took from the pot in the centre of the table and sprinkled into his mug. He left the debris on the table-top, fiddling with the empty papers, folding the tubes in half, and then in half again. She watched him stirring without looking down as he spoke at speed.

She told him she'd worked hard in the restaurant and

built up a great business in down town Stuart. The kids were all grown-up and gone and settled in upstate New York. There were three grandchildren. All girls. Little darlings they were, though she didn't see as much of them as she'd like to, especially since her husband had passed and she'd had some health issues, she said, making quote marks with her fingers around 'issues'. She'd sold the restaurant; but she'd kept the house. With the girls coming, she was happy it would be full again.

They keyed each other's numbers into their cell phones and agreed it would be good to meet up again once Christmas was done and their families had headed home.

"Call me, honey" she said, as she started up the truck in the parking lot, her soft North Carolina drawl lingering in his head long after she disappeared from view.

❧

He texted her the day he took the tree down. He looked around his condo. January empty. He reached under the bed and took his Gibson out of its velvet-lined case, as though he was removing a dead loved one from a coffin. He plugged in his earphones and began to pick along to the Bob Marley backing track. But it did little to lift his mood.

In readiness for Melissa's visit, he turned the condo balcony into a magic grotto: light, linen drapes that kept out the full sunlight and swayed gently in the wind. He adorned the popcorn walls with rare shells – left-handed whelks mostly – and sharks' teeth which he combed from the shoreline. On the table top, he placed bleached sand dollars, perfectly intact, lily-side-up, and finds of smoothed, red and green sea glass, along with the champagne flutes.

She arrived in a simple little black dress that covered up her arms and shoulders and all the other bits of her she didn't much like anymore. Her fair-grey hair was freshly washed, its fringe thatched her face. She'd had her roots done.

He got out his black, silk shirt and pants, and dressed himself just as he did when he still played bass, on occasion, with the guys in the reggae band. Those who were left of them from the old days. He made sure to cover up his grey parting with henna.

"You know, honey, I'd rather eat in than go to Conchy Joe's Place," she said, after they'd had more than a few glasses of champagne. "If you got some spare pants and a T-shirt, I'll fix us something to eat."

He liked the look of her in his joggers and hoodie as she stood at the counter chopping scallions and zucchini and cilantro. He admired her knife skills. His kitchen smelled unfamiliar with the garlic and the simmering of wine in the open pan. He breathed in the sheer warmth of it all.

"Need feeding up, honey. Gonna put some meat on those bones of yours," she told him as they sat down to the pasta.

If it wasn't for the pasta, then he probably wouldn't have suggested that she be his house-mate and she wouldn't have thought it a good idea. He needed someone to share the rent. Oceanfront condos didn't come cheap. She needed the company. She was rattling around in the empty house in Stuart. She'd offer it to the realtor as a short-term let. They'd let things run.

She installed furniture from her town house – a taupe sofa to replace his shabby one; the beech dining table and six matching chairs and the family dresser where she displayed her dinner service and photographs of her family. She brought her own bed and pillows for the spare room.

Greg stood in his condo and wondered if he lived there anymore. It wasn't that he didn't like the look of it; but he knew he'd have to be over-careful not to leave things about on surfaces, not to make a mess in the diner, not to flick ash onto the balcony, not to leave the seat up in the John, not to leave coffee stains on the side tables.

But she was a great cook and he wondered what it was about him that attracted women who felt obliged to feed him up. Not that he minded. As January moved into February and into March, she fed him rib-eye and filet mignon, venison and veal. Night after night, she piled his plate high with salad and fresh vegetables and stuffed him full of deserts: brulé and key lime and her home-made apple pie just like her Mom used to make. No more TV dinners.

Every day at dawn he still upped and went fishing on the beach out front. Melissa packed his cooler box with shrimp and jumbo prawn threaded on cocktails sticks, and muffins and rum-balls sprinkled with desiccated coconut. *Just to keep you going, honey*, she said.

After he left, she'd sit on the balcony with a coffee and a cigarette and watch him standing on the strandline with the sanderlings, casting out his line. He reminded her of the little birds, skinny little legs that skittered along the shore with a restlessness that made her tired with the looking. She often wondered what he thought about all day, what he was looking for out there on the horizon, the Gulf Stream shimmering in the distance. But she didn't ask.

As the weeks passed, she could see that the knotted veins in his torso and forearms were not standing so proud, that his waistline was thickening ever so slightly, that his baggies didn't hang so low on his hips. She wondered if the adage about the way to a man's heart was true.

When she wasn't cooking, she was hitting the beach to walk, heading northwards where the people were fewer, striding along the shore, arms like pistons, until she felt she'd faded away in the heat haze.

"Gotta shed these pounds, honey" she told Greg. "Can't have you all thin and brown and me like an old, beached manatee."

She avoided staking out in the Floridian sun, instead spraying herself with fast-tan. She got her navel pierced with a diamond which glinted in the intense light. She had manicures, pedicures and her nails painted in pink shellac polish at the Vietnamese nail bar in the Treasure Coast Mall. She wore a silver bracelet around her left ankle that jingled when she moved. She maintained the discipline of the power-walking and by June, she'd shed the pounds and was down to 120. She didn't feel like the self she had become over the last few years. At least most of the time. Yet despite the piercing, and the deep mahogany tan, and the jewellery that tinkled, she still couldn't step into her bikini or swimsuit. As she walked, her fingers tugged at her vest top for fear it would expose the scar where her right breast used to be.

When she'd done with walking, she'd be back in the comfort of the kitchen, cooking or polishing the condo. It shone and smelled of a potent mix of fried onions and Mr Sheen. Nowhere was a speck of dust allowed to settle.

And every evening at dusk, when Greg finally came off the beach, he brought her a love offering of pompano which she wrapped tenderly in foil and baked in the oven.

In early August, Melissa turned fifty-eight. Greg was, what he termed, *cooking*, in celebration: dips and finger foods, pretzels and chips which he set out in bowls and platters on the little table on the balcony. They sat on the Adirondack chairs and laughed, sipping margaritas through straws from glasses with salt-encrusted rims. Greg took out his leather pouch and placed the weed intently along his cigarette paper, easing the contents into position with his fingers. He rolled-up, licked along the edge to seal before lighting-up.

Melissa watched him take the first drag, sucking in so hard that the hollows of his cheeks must have been almost touching on the inside. All scooped out.

He handed her the joint to share, but she shook her head and gestured with her hand for added emphasis.

"You okay me, here?" she asked.

"It's good," he said, and carried on smoking. "I'm cool with it all."

If it wasn't for the fact that it was Melissa's birthday and maybe the dope, then perhaps Greg wouldn't have leaned across and kissed her on the lips for the first time and asked her if she'd like to share his bed.

Later, they'd slept like babies, Melissa snuggled up to Greg's back. She always felt cold in the air con, she said. She draped her arms around his slightly swelling belly and tucked her knees into the back of his. She liked the feel of skin against skin, her cheek in his hair.

When he'd asked, she'd told him about the mastectomy and he'd traced her scar with the tips of the fingers of his left hand. His guitar-plucking hand. They'd felt rough on her flesh.

When she'd asked, he'd told her that the *Nina* etched in ink alongside the green-scaled mermaid tattoo on his right buttock, didn't mean anything to him anymore.

And in the morning, as usual, he'd gone fishing before she woke. She lay in bed for a while, looking at the feathered dreamcatcher that was tacked to the post on his side of the bed and wondered what troubled his sleep so badly that he needed to spirit his nightmares away.

Melissa was apprehensive, yet excited, to host Greg's family for Thanksgiving. It was the first time they'd made, what she called a statement to them about Greg and her being a couple. In the condo kitchen she felt in control, more so than she'd felt in years, prepping the turkey, peeling the vegetables, simmering the cranberries, stirring the gravy. She loved setting the table for a get-together like this. There were tea lights, fine linen place mats and matching napkins, the best eating-irons and crockery. The full works. And there was Greg's daughter, Carla, her husband, Doug, and their little girl, Martha, sitting beside them in the high-chair.

Melissa liked being in the wings in the kitchen and enjoyed the fact that her labour resulted in everyone having a good time. For a few moments, she thought of her husband, and being back in the restaurant business in Stuart, working as a team behind the scenes, looking at guests she hardly knew at all, watching the conversation and the wine flow.

But when she finally settled herself down at the table, she felt like an imposter. As she turned to Greg, she saw for the first time that he talked without drawing breath, holding court to a captive audience about the size of the last pompano he'd caught, or how he and the band could still draw a crowd at the Sunday morning farmers' market waterside in Stuart, or how he still made a buck or two dabbling in the stock markets. What he didn't tell them was that he'd recently developed a fear of heights and had put it to Melissa that they try and rent a condo on the ground floor now that they were officially an item.

She watched him as if everything was back to front, him stabbing the turkey with that left hand of his. He filled his glass brim-full with red wine before seeing to anyone else. She marked his drinking pace, speeding up with every glass. She noted the red stains on the white cloth and thought about how she'd have trouble getting them out in the laundry, whether she'd have to use bleach, how many cycles she'd have to put the washer on, and if they'd ever be fully lifted out. It was then that Nina came up.

"D'you ever, see her? Nina? That bitch of a mother of yours?" Greg asked Carla.

"If you mean, Mom, Greg. Yes, I do."

Melissa suddenly understood a large part of this family history in just those two brief utterances.

They finished dinner pretty quickly after that and Melissa insisted they watch TV and try and relax while she cleared away. She was the host, after all. She put the dishes in the washer on the longest cycle, wiped the surfaces down, returned everything meticulously to its proper place. They should just chill out, she said. Tomorrow they'd all be going home.

If it wasn't for the fact that Greg's family overslept because little Martha had been running a temperature, then Greg wouldn't have offered to drive them all south back to Lauderdale the day after Thanksgiving. He said it wouldn't put him out at all, and it was the least he could do. He'd take the opportunity to stop over, see some old friends, hit the malls. He'd be back in a couple of days.

After they'd packed up and left, Melissa sat in the condo, looking at her furniture. It didn't seem to fit in the way it did in the old house at Stuart. She opened up the sliders to let the warmth of the humid air seep into her before she sat down, lit up, and inhaled deeply. She gazed at the snowbirds along the strandline and wondered how they knew the exact moment to arrive, the exact moment to take flight. It was clever programming, she reckoned, just as she knew when the rubbing had to stop when she was making gingerbread men.

After she finished her cigarette she raised herself from the chair, walked to the thermostat in the lobby and turned off the air con. She left the sliders open. Her bones seemed colder since she'd undergone treatment for the cancer and even colder since her husband had died. She liked the fact she could control the temperature with a quick flick of the dial now she had the condo to herself for a couple of days. It must be similar to the feeling Greg got when he took ownership of the remote for the TV and watched Bloomberg.

She went into the kitchen and opened the larder unit, took out the flour, sugar, cinnamon, ginger and currants and placed them on the counter. She opened the fridge and got out the butter. From the drawer, she took her rolling pin and cutter. She was ready then.

She stood in the kitchen rubbing the mixture, listening to the rhythm of the waves through the sliders and watching the drapes at the windows billow in the breeze. As ever, the dough was perfect and she rolled it out and took the cutter, pressing out the gingerbread men, and lifting them gently one-by-one onto the baking tray which she placed in the oven.

She sat drinking a coffee at the diner-bar while they baked, the aroma filling the condo, and her, with comfort. Her husband fleetingly seemed present. She touched her vest top and put her hand on her scar; but it was his fingers she felt tracing its slightly raised surface. The fingers of his right hand. They felt smooth on her crinkly flesh.

As soon as the baking had cooled on the rack, she lined

a tin with parchment and placed a delicate white doily on the base. She layered the gingerbread men on top, tucked them in tightly with the paper, and then sealed the tin.

It was dusk on the Sunday when Greg pulled into his space in the parking lot. With his arms laden with shopping finds for Melissa in readiness for their first Christmas together, he entered the elevator and pressed the button for the sixth floor. He stepped out, walking quietly along the outside walkway towards the entrance of the condo.

He'd got used to the familiar waft of cooking welcoming him in from the beach so it was the absence of any kind of smell that first made his stomach lurch. He fumbled in his pocket for the key and opened the door. Inside all was dark. He groped for the light switch in the lobby. Gone was the dresser with the photographs and the best china dinner service. Gone was the dining table and the six matching chairs. All that remained was the 26-inch plasma screen, the remote control, and a stainless steel ashtray, full to overflowing, on top of the occasional side table at the side of his chair, where she'd placed the tin of freshly-baked gingerbread men.

Asking For It

CONDITIONS ARE PERFECT: the buffalo shit is compacting under the overhead sun, baked into honey-coloured concrete across the savannahs of Sabi Sabi. The appetising stench of young kudu kill clogs the air, the darkening carrion congealing glutinously as the afternoon glares on. Some vultures perch sleepy and sated in an acacia somewhere on the horizon, every so often a chilling caw echoes across the plain.

Deep in the flesh under the ridge of the black beast you are riding, you're tasting a new life. Good. Evil. After all, a parasite's life carries no stigma for you: you are happy to live life off the backs of others; but you soon will have had your fill here. Fresh flesh will beckon from the bush beyond.

You've always thought of yourself as simply opportunistic – an any host will do sort of approach to life – but now feels different. Overnight it has been crispy cold over the grasslands under the clear and starlit southern sky, but dawn saw the sun, a blood orange, rise with the certainty that it would be dripping hot by mid-morning. These vagaries in temperature triggered changes in you that were temperamental and uncertain, made you react instinctively to stimulus.

You can sense him there down at the water hole. You can feel his body heat through the screen of sand flies and reeds that are choking the water, imagine the toasty smokiness of his breath. He is exhaling, moistening the lenses of his Ralph Lauren sunglasses and then polishing them with a bright blue cloth taken from the breast pocket of his jacket. For bush walking, he is wearing *inappropriate* clothing if he wants to keep safe from pests such as you – thin, linen, above-the-knee khaki shorts straight out of the club-house scene from 'Out of Africa.' He resembles a mix of Colonial Master and Robert Redford. And he's doused himself in that strongly scented aftershave, sandalwood or some other exotic spice. What with the shorts and the scent, he is surely sending out overt signals, appealing to your basest instinct. Asking for it.

You psych yourself up ready for the silent attack. Let those who want to refer to you pejoratively as *just a mite* or *some bothersome little tick* carry on; they are just words. You are confident in your power and potency; you'll show them, taking you for a fool like that, show them that you have the most malignant and malevolent of motives; that you, just an eight-legged blood-sucking parasitic arthropod can inflict pain they could never imagine. And make *him* wish he'd stuck to the *Deet*.

He doesn't see you – or feel you – as you gently blow close on the breeze without a whisper, and on up through the billow of his shorts, brushing the hairs on his tanned, sun-screen slathered thighs. You linger a few moments in the creases and moistness of his sweaty groin, savouring the thought of the warm blood that is so close. And so, most methodically and with great intent, you attach yourself to his penis, carefully inserting your razor-sharp mandibles into the tip and then rapturously sinking your tooth-covered feeding tube into the skin.

It is true: that first taste is like no other; that first bite; that first suck; and that first slurp of the rich delicacy that is human blood. Perfect mammalian warmth as you engorge your depleted body and drink until you have your fill. About time. You think of it as nothing more than an exchange of gifts: his blood to you, your saliva with all the diseased bounty of your former hosts, just for him. You nestle in your new and generous host and play out the days to come.

Your host will enjoy his lovely few hours alone at the watering hole – he'll observe the hippos lazing, slimily submerged in brown-grey mud; he might feel slightly perturbed at the crocodiles, perhaps a little too close for comfort; he'll certainly swat away the monotonous murmurings of mosquitoes hovering in clouds over the dank water. But he won't notice little old you.

It will be when he gets back to the comfort of the lodge after his afternoon on foot, when he'll be taking his outdoor shower, listening for the call of the exotic blue korhaan and anticipating his sundowner that he might notice, just a simple old little tick, black, in amongst the white suds where you will be lying in repose, fed and fat and replete. *I wonder how that got there,* he might say, *no bother.* And he'll remove you, unhooking you with his firm, yet careful tug, discarding you like a seed on the wind into the African sunset. He won't give the moment a second thought.

You fast forward six days. He'll be back to the reassuring comfort of home when the fever sets in. You can see him alone is his crisp, white, cotton bed sheets, his skin, cabbage-red in contrast. Temperature and fear are combining to make him sweat profusely, pouring off his brow along the strained creases of his face. His usually slick, groomed hair now a sodden mop. The headaches are blinding, like the white light that's flooding the room. And the tell-tale pustular eruptions of the tick typhus you carry, the colour of the *Germolene* he will be spreading, are pocking his torso. And he will breathe in that distinctive odour, an odour he has never smelled before, that peculiar sweet and pungent aroma of rottenness and decay.

What a pity, you would say if you could feel any sympathy anymore, *what a pity* that his aching body is contorting – that will be the abdominal cramps and that wretched watery diarrhoea. The juddering is so strong that the glass he is trying to hold is clinking against his incisors and canines as he tries to steady it with hands, weak and chilled with cold. Yes, his extremities are glacier-cold – his fingers, his toes, his cyanising lips. And he thinks of his penis and recalls that evening in the shower and that bothersome little tick and reaches frantically beneath the sheets. Deep in the soft hidden flesh, all he will see are your signature crusty scabs. Just a little souvenir from a once-in-a-lifetime safari. Yes, things are progressing as perfectly as you envisage and you will continue to relish this newly found turpitude and moral corruption.

May he never be purged nor cured by death
but his crisis be long and lingering,
his penitence painful.

Imitation Daisies

THE ARMCHAIR IS just there at high water mark among
the driftwood, bladder wrack and mermaids' purses.
The brown leather is faded and cracked, stuffing worming
out of the seat, yet its arms are reaching out for him. Tom
eases himself into its embrace. Takes a breather. The weight
off his legs.

He glances at his wrist watch. Still only 05:00. Not everyone has trouble sleeping. He bends forward and unlaces his
trainers, pulls off his socks and places them on the damp
sand at the side of the chair. He rolls up his jogger bottoms
to just below the knee, his long-sleeved T-shirt to just below
the elbow. His bare soles feel good on the sand: connected.
The early morning August sun from behind, goes some
way to warm his body from the outside in.

He leans his head against the back-rest, stretches out
his hands and spreads his fingers across the arms, tries to
relax. He feels drained, too exhausted to switch off. What
Morwenna used to call *over-tired*. It's been this way since
she's gone, so every new day forces him to walk in the
hope that he will sink into a sleep so deep that he might
never wake up.

The wings of the chair obscure his view to either side so he gazes directly out in front of him at the ebbing tide and the wisps of cumulus clouds on the horizon. The lazy rhythm of the waves is soothing and he tries to regulate his breathing, as he's been shown, to keep time with their constant motion: in, two, three, four. Out, two, three, four.

He closes his eyes and attempts to drift, but it's Morwenna's face that rushes in. That lopsided smile. That slightly crooked tooth. The sloping eyebrows that always made her look so sad. The face doesn't have an age that he can pinpoint as young Morwenna, or old Morwenna, or somewhere in-between Morwenna, it is just the essence of her: the ageless truth of Morwenna.

He opens his eyes and out there, way beyond the shorebreak, he sees a figure slicing through the water. It's moving from right to left across his field of vision, making splashes with every stroke of the arms, every kick of the feet. But it's the small, orange flash of colour that's bobbing above the surface that brings him to.

He settles himself back down into what already seem to be familiar arms, taking some comfort from the well-worn hide and the sheer shabbiness of it all, like him, washed-up and washed-out, stranded on a shoreline between high and low tide. He sinks down into the damaged cushion, burrowing into the seclusion and intimacy of this private space that's been gifted to him for the time being

His attempt to relax is disrupted once again by the re-appearance of the orange cap, like a marker buoy, punctuating the smooth surface of the water far beyond the breaking waves. He sits upright, leans his neck forward, strains his eyes to try and see more of this bather. The figure is too distant to be defined, to see the features of the face under-neath the fluorescent cap, see flesh on the bones of the body which is cutting through the water with direction and grace. Yet like him, the person who is out there, beyond his recognition, is drawn by the sea when the rest of the world is tucked up in bed still sleeping.

If he were thinking straight he'd know that this couldn't possibly be Morwenna. She is dead, for God's sake. He'd covered her white legs with a blue-waffled, hospital blanket in a feeble attempt to keep them warm when they were stone cold and lifeless. And anyway, no-one had loathed the water more than she had. It was only an occasional dip, when the tide happened to be full at the end of a long summer's day. Only then, when the sun had warmed the sand would she wallow in the shallows, wearing that foul swim-cap for fear that the waves would spoil her hair. She would never go out of her depth, always staying inside the shore-break. Sometimes she feigned breaststroke, moving her arms in perfect circles; but her feet never left the ground. He knew that for sure.

But now he's not so sure of anything. Grief and lack of sleep have put him in a frame of mind poised somewhere between here and elsewhere. It's a fuzzy place of magical thinking and disconnection that his friends have told him will fade with time, just as the indistinct shape out in the bay is disappearing towards the east.

As the moon tugs at the tide, the beach pulls him back, earlier and earlier each passing day, the crack of dawn light breaking the long, sleepless dark, and muscle-memory instructing his feet to walk, and propel him along the sand to the armchair that's sitting there waiting as if just for him.

As the time dawdles by, he notices that the leather is changing: to the touch and to the eye, stiffening and bleaching with the prolonged sunshine and salt air. But it still welcomes him, accommodates his aching soul, and gives some sort of sustenance for his hollowness.

He's scans the water for the swimmer. Wills it to appear, wondering if he can conjure it up with the looking, and at the same time realises what he is actually hoping for is absolutely beyond logic. But this morning the figure doesn't appear. The beach and the ocean are empty. Just miles of nothingness. And a heaviness on his chest that he thinks will crush him.

He lets himself fall back into the chair and into a state that resembles sleep. It's not unconsciousness, but a safe place where his eyes are shuttered and the world blotted out. All that remains is the sound of the waves lapping and the herring gulls squealing overhead. The faintest offshore breeze is brushing his forearms: he can feel the hairs stand on end. He's absorbed by all this feeling. And with this feeling comes a sudden cold, wetness on his left elbow as it rests on the chair arm.

Without opening his eyes, he touches his cheeks with his right hand, wondering if, for the first time in months, he is shedding tears. But his cheeks are dry. He opens his eyes and shifts his gaze left. And there she is in her orange cap, standing shivering in her sensible bathing costume. Drips from the bunch of rubber daisies are raining on to his forearm.

"Sorry," she says. "Didn't mean to wake you."

"I wasn't sleeping," he says. "Just daydreaming."

He looks at her body, planted there on the sand beside him. It seems solid enough: good strong bones holding it together like the wooden ribs of shipwrecks that lie half-buried along this Atlantic-facing beach. Though her skin is paler than he remembers it: bloodless, tinged blue, veins visible, and slightly puffy, with a translucence like the jellyfish he sometimes sees stranded on the tide drop. But perhaps that's the cold. God knows how long she's been in the water.

"I'm freezing," she says. "Been in for ages."

"Here, let me rub you down. Warm you up a bit," he says.

"You'll have a job," she laughs.

He rises from the chair and bends to pick up his striped beach towel which he has weighted down with his sandals. He wraps it around her and starts to buff her shoulders, her back, the tops of her thighs, her calves. Tries to get the circulation going. He can't seem to warm her. And she feels different to the touch, as though if he were to rub her too hard with the towel, he would erase her completely.

When he's done, he drapes the towel across her shoulders but she makes no attempt to make a shawl of it. It just hangs on her framework, the stripes running vertically from neck to knee.

They stand facing each other not knowing quite what to say. Tom finds it hard to believe that it's only a month since she died. It seems like a lot longer.

"I didn't see you swimming earlier," he says. "I've been looking for you, hoping it was you, though didn't know it actually was you. It was just a feeling."

"I was swimming in a different direction this morning,"

she says. "And it really is me. I've been watching you too. Sorry sight you are here every day, on your own, hanging around moping"

"Haven't been able to do much."

"I can see that," she says. "Only natural, I suppose."

"But I can see you're doing okay. Taken up swimming?"

"Yes. Long distance."

"But you never liked swimming."

"I was afraid before. But now I'm not afraid of anything. And anyway, I wanted to try something new."

"You never said."

"No. I never said."

"But the hat? I hate that hat. Always have."

There's a puckering of rubber as she unpeels the swim-cap from her head and places it on the arm of the chair.

"Don't let me forget it," she says.

"I won't," he says.

Tom watches as she shakes her hair free of the tight, orange hat. It's still thick and wavy as it was when she was young, but now it's grey. A steel-white grey that tumbles down past her shoulders almost to her waist. It's bone dry. Unspoiled. Just as she wanted it to be.

"You still have a beautiful head of hair, you know," he says.

"Always was my crowning glory," she says. "But you never seemed to notice."

He stretches out his right hand to touch her hair, and for a brief moment attempts to twist his fingers though the curls. They don't feel as they look; they're brittle, like wire-wool. She laughs and reaches out her hand to touch his; but he can't feel the contact even though he can see her fingers stroking the raised veins on the back of his hand, in front of his very eyes.

"Can you stay?" he asks. "For a little while?"

"Sorry, but no, I can't. For the first time ever, I've found something I really want to do. I'm in my element in the water."

"Didn't waste any time, then?"

"No. And neither should you."

"But I'm lost without you, you know."

"I know that. It'll pass."

"I didn't know you could be so cold, Morwenna."

"Lots you never knew about me, Tom," she says.

And then she drops the towel and picks her way across the shingle, her feet not seeming to react to the jagged razor shells, the desiccated seaweed, the stiffened star fish and dislocated crab claws. She turns her head, just once, and lifts her arm to wave at him before stepping into the ocean. He watches the back of her, as she slips, inch my inch, into the waiting sea, like a silver mermaid.

Tom sits back down. He's mesmerised by the water. He knows in less than a few days, the ocean will encroach way past the damp expanse in front of him, eat into the fine grains of dry sand, surge once again up to the high water mark beneath the dunes where his chair remains beached for the moment. He imagines the successive waves as they'll lap at his ankles, lick at his calves. He imagines his chair losing its anchorage as the ocean makes a boat of it and floats it out to sea. But for the time being, he holds the orange swim-cap in his hands, feeling the raised cluster of imitation daisies.

Torn Ligaments

D AD CALLS ME to say Mum's had a bit of a mishap. No need to go into overdrive and catastrophise as I normally do. She's all in one piece; though she's come a bit of a cropper and had a nasty fall down the stairs. It could have been a lot worse but she's fine now and comfortable in the bed downstairs.

I see her through the window as I walk up the path. She's in a single bed that's been placed next to the window. She's propped up with pillows. Normally, when she's what she terms, *herself,* and in residence, she has the air of someone about to grant an audience with a subservient being of her realm. But she doesn't look very regal or powerful. She seems lost.

For the first time in years I don't feel confrontational. What's the point? I'll do small talk, I vow. Just let her be. She's ninety-two-years-of-age with a knackered ankle and torn ligaments for God's sake.

She smiles when I come in and I notice her eyes are full. She doesn't say anything but as usual offers me her cheek to kiss. She pats the blanket and invites me to sit beside her on the edge of the bed. I do as I am told. I feel like a child again. A sixty-seven-year-old child on a mother's bed, frightened that she's slipping away.

I'm four-years-old and I'm back where we lived above the butcher's shop. It's a late February evening. My brother, he-of-the-middle-name, Peter James, has just been born and I've been invited into the bedroom to see him for the first time. Until then, I've been sitting on the landing, shut outside, listening at the door, feeling very cold and lonelier than usual.

Inside the bedroom it's unusually warm. The coal fire has been lit especially and is still burning strong in the grate. Dad takes the poker and riddles the ash through, picks up the hod and throws on more coal, covering it with a layer of ashes to bank the fire so it keeps going through the night. He pulls the curtains shut. There is condensation running down the inside of the windows.

Mum is sitting up in bed, smiling. There's a glow on her face – peachy – like the lamp shade with the tassels on the bedside table. But it's as though there is a glow that's coming from somewhere inside her that's not just because of the heat in the room or the ambience created by the peachy light. She has an expression on her face that I've rarely seen before. I instantly make the connection with the baby – my new brother – who's wrapped tightly in a white crocheted shawl and is sucking at her breast. She looks content. Fulfilled.

She pats the purple-quilted eiderdown and asks me with her dark eyes to sit on the bed. Begrudgingly, I do as I'm asked. There is a sickly-sweet smell in the air, not from her as yet undiagnosed, diabetic breath, not from the Teachers she will turn to when I'm thirteen after her step mother takes her own life; but from the very pores of her skin. I breathe it in as I edge closer: sweat and Imperial Leather and wet flannel and Yardley and watery colostrum as she suckles this thing at her breast. Even though she puts her free arm around me and draws me into her warm body, I feel her slipping away. Already I sense that she will find it easier to love this new baby than me. If it is possible to feel grief for the first time – without someone being dead – this is the moment.

I ask Mum if, and when, she feels up to it, she'd like me to take her out for a run in the car to have a change of scenery and some fresh air. This is a first for me. I know what's brought it on. If I'm honest, I don't want her to die and leave me feeling guilty. I'm aware she knows I'm trying to play the good and dutiful daughter, a role that is completely out of character.

She doesn't say no simply for the sake of saying no this time. She seems open to my suggestion. Not effusive or excited. But as though she'll oblige. Humour me.

"I'd like go to Oxwich, she says. "It's not far, I know. But far enough with the ankle and the weakness at this age."

"That's strange," I reply. "I was thinking the exact same thing."

"Well, there we are then," she says.

❧

A few days later, she's at the ready, sitting on the edge of the bed, lipstick on, hair combed. She is tapping her fingers over and over on the top of the walking stick that Dad has fashioned for her out of a lovely piece of elm in his shed. My stomach tightens and it feels our roles are being reversed: that today I am to be mother to a dependent, though petulant, offspring.

I link arms with her and hoist her off the bed. She's lost weight, seems to be shrinking before my eyes. She tells me that she can manage very well, just as she always has, without my help, thank you very much. She makes her way slowly across the living room, through the kitchen, and down the steps where the handrail has been installed by the occupational therapy team. I tell her to watch out, to be careful on the path because the fallen leaves are making it slippery. She tells me she's not a child as she forges her way to the car outside. She waves at Dad who's standing inside, peeping over the nets in the front window, looking at us both go off on this mission into uncharted territory.

I give her a leg up into the 4 x 4, her tutting about the fact that we still have this *truck*, as she calls it, after all that has happened. She never talks about my accident and how I nearly died in my own drive. It's one of those subjects that are best left alone. A bit like my Dad's butcher's knives that despite what happened to Mum's step-mother, came with them from the shop when they retired to the cottage back in the village where Mum was born. Dad had hoped it would be a new start. He never stops hoping.

I keep schtum. Through the years, Mum and I have

found it better to avoid our pasts which, despite the agreed silence, are tacked like shadows to our heels. Today, I'm going to keep my big mouth shut and see what happens. As Dad has always told me, *don't go upsetting your mother.* It is the mantra we have always lived by. And he's always told me that it isn't that my mother doesn't love me; it's that she just has a funny way of showing it and doesn't like my *ways.*

I help her in, bottom first, and then lift her legs after her and place them in the passenger well. I close the door. Sealed up front with me, it's not dissimilar to having my one of my three granddaughters with me. My dependants. Apart from the smell of old age rather than the fresh scent of children.

"I'm glad we're going to Oxwich," I say. "Good choice. Looks like the weather's going to hold for a while, too, so let's make the most of it, shall we?"

"Yes," she says. The forecast's not looking good for later. Better get going to get back."

The car park at Oxwich Bay is empty apart from our *truck.* No-one at the gate charging a £6 entry fee. No-one outside the restaurant which is having building work done. Not a soul on the beach. It has a beautiful out-of-season feel. And it's all ours.

We park up as close as is possible to the beach, where the flat gravel meets the gentle slope of smooth pebbles. The golden sand and almost-full tide is shimmering in the soft light of late September.

"It's lovely here in the mornings," I say. "Loses the light fast, though, doesn't it?"

"Mmm. That's why we always used to try and get here early, your father and I, so that we could make the most of it when you were young. Where do the years go?" she says.

"I know," I say. "Seems like nothing has changed and yet everything has changed."

"Do you remember when that hotel was the Old Rectory?" she asks, looking in the direction of the Oxwich Bay Hotel.

"Course I do," I say. "Kept *JAPET* in the woods right next door."

"Happy times," she says. "You and Peter, when you were kids."

"Yes, happy times. Even though you didn't give me a middle name," I say. "Plain Jane."

"You didn't look as if you needed one," she says. "You didn't seem to be calling out for a bit of your grandmothers to carry you through life."

"Is that a compliment?"

"I'm just saying, that's all. Anyway, do you remember singing, 'We all live in a yellow submarine' when we were in the boat? Your father at the tiller of *JAPET*?" she asks.

"Course I do."

And all of a sudden we break into song, her in a deep bass, probably because of her deafness, and me out of tune and crackling because of my sinus issues. We give it our all and when we stop, our girlish laughter fills the truck.

"I didn't mean to neglect you, you know," she says, staring through the windscreen, straight ahead at the ocean beyond.

"I know you didn't, Mum."

"I tried to do my best but . . ."

I interrupt her and say that there's no need to explain. We all do what we can at the time. It's all any of us can do. I tell her that I'll probably be having the same conversation with my kids at some time, as they will with their children.

That's mothers and kids. I know she wants me to say, *You've been a good mother* as much as I want her to say, *You've been a good daughter.* But neither of us can let ourselves do this. Instead I ask her if she fancies a little paddle, let the salt water soothe her feet, tell her that in September the sea is at its warmest. She tells me she knows that without me having to explain. *I might be old, but I've still got my marbles, you know,* she reminds me.

We walk the short distance to the slipway where we used to launch *JAPET.* I offer her my arm and she takes it as we pick away down the concrete and on to the damp sand. She rests her hands on my shoulders to keep her balance while I stoop down and help her off with her shoes and socks and roll up her trousers. She places her stick on the slipway along with her shoes and socks and we step into the ocean near the rocks where the trees run down to the sea. We don't say anything, but wade, calf-high through the gentle shore-break, the weak sun in our faces as we lean into each other for support.

How long we walk like this, I don't know. It seems timeless. All the years melding into this moment as we plod through the shallows, retracing the steps we've taken over our lifetimes, the limestone cliffs at Tor Point beckoning in the distance. Here in the silence between us, I can sense it is the same for her too. This feeling of time passing.

And then she's says that, sorry, she can't go any further. That's it. She's tired. She feels the weather's about to turn. She can sense it in her bones and she doesn't want me getting soaked through and catching a chill.

"We'd better be making tracks. Your father will be worried about me. Afraid that my sugars will go low and

I won't be back in time for lunch. You know what he's like. I don't know what I'd do without him."

I hear those very same words echo down the years. Mum has taken to her bed, yet again, and Dad's saying: *Don't know what I'd do without you. Especially the way things are.*

We head back to the slipway and I ease her down on to the concrete. I towel her feet dry, get the sand from between her toes. She tells me to be extra careful with her feet because of the diabetes, and that she's proud of her feet, that she's always had good feet and hopes that the torn ligaments won't complicate things. She's seen some terrible states on diabetics' feet. I tell her I haven't forgotten about the diabetes or the feet. How could I? So I use the towel extra gently, conscious of the sand's abrasive action on skin so fragile that I could rub it raw or buff her away. I put her socks back on and then, what she calls, the sensible shoes that Dad has insisted she wears these days. I do up the Velcro on the upper of the right one; the left, I leave unstuck to accommodate the foot that is still tender and slightly swollen.

Back in the truck, I put the demister on to clear the front windscreen and set the wipers to low speed because of the rain that's started to speck the glass. We sit looking out over the bay, watching the approaching front as we drink tea from the Thermos flask I have brought. I've made it milky, just as she likes it, even though I've always insisted on having mine black, weak, just a dip of the tea bag.

"I knew we were in for a change," she says.

"You're usually right about the weather. I'll give you that much at least."

"There are worse things in life than bad weather and a spot of rain. You know that as well as I do. We just have to get on with these things as best we can."

I feel four years-of-age again, a little girl sitting on the landing outside the bedroom door, waiting for the instruction to come in and sit on the bed with a pat of a hand. I reach for that same hand now, clinging onto the tiny fingers, longing to feel just the slightest squeeze in return. Some kind of connection.

Acknowledgements

T HANKS TO CHRIS and the team at Salt for reinvesting in me and this second collection of short fiction which I'm honoured to take to market with them. To Nicholas Royle and the Manchester Fiction Prize who saw seeds of potential in my short fiction from my early writing in 2011 to the present day – many of my highly commended stories appear in this collection as does 'Connective Tissue', the title story, which made the final in 2017. I thank them for truly valuing the short story genre and for giving me increasing confidence as a young writer in the fullest sense of the word.

Thanks to the wonderful Irish writer and mentor, Claire Keegan, for her inspiration and the impetus to try and write quietly. Thanks to all the friends I made through the Hay Writers at Work Creative Development Bursary 2018 and 2019 – their continuing friendship is appreciated. To the community of writers at the Creative Writing Department, Swansea University, whose ongoing interest in my development is second-to-none – special thanks to Elaine Canning, Alan Bilton and Carole Hailey. Diolch yn fawr iawn to Jon Gower, writer and academic, who first introduced me to the possibilities of the short story – many of the stories in this collection had their genesis under his wing at Swansea University back in 2011. Thanks too, to John Lavin, writer, academic and editor of the wonderful, *The Lonely Crowd*, for the opportunities he has given me both as a writer, and more recently as a guest editor. My appreciation goes to all my Twitter friends in the UK, USA, and Australia for their encouragement. It keeps me going. And to the West Cork Literary Festival and the Cultural Institute, Swansea University for the many wonderful Zooms during the darkest days of lockdowns, the authors kept me sane and connected to writing and I don't know what I would have done without them.

Finally, to TSS Publishing, Retreat West, Accent Press, The London Magazine, and The Swansea Review who previously published earlier versions of stories that appear in this collection, and to BBC Radio 4 who first broadcast 'Soft Boiled Eggs' in 2022 as part of its *Short Works* series.

This book has been typeset by
SALT PUBLISHING LIMITED
using Granjon, a font designed by George W. Jones
for the British branch of the Linotype company in the
United Kingdom. It is manufactured using Holmen
Book Cream 70gsm, a Forest Stewardship Council™
certified paper from the Hallsta Paper Mill in Sweden.
It was printed and bound by Clays Limited in Bungay,
Suffolk, Great Britain.

CROMER
GREAT BRITAIN
MMXXII